POST-APOCALYPTIC VEHICULAR MAYHEM

GASLANDS
REFUELLED

MIKE HUTCHINSON

OSPREY
GAMES

OSPREY GAMES

Bloomsbury Publishing Plc

PO Box 883, Oxford, OX1 9PL, UK

1385 Broadway, 5th Floor, New York, NY 10018, USA

E-mail: info@ospreygames.co.uk

www.ospreygames.co.uk

OSPREY GAMES is a trademark of Osprey Publishing Ltd

First published in Great Britain in 2019

A catalogue record for this book is available from the British Library.

ISBN: HB 9781472838834;
 eBook 9781472838872;
ePDF 9781472838865;
XML 9781472838889

19 20 21 22 23 10 9 8 7 6 5 4 3 2 1

Originated by PDQ Digital Media Solutions, Bungay, UK
Printed in China by C&C Offset Printing Co., Ltd.

Osprey Games supports the Woodland Trust, the UK's leading woodland conservation charity.

To find out more about our authors and books visit www.ospreygames.co.uk. Here you will find extracts, author interviews, details of forthcoming events and the option to sign up for our newsletter.

AUTHOR
Mike Hutchinson is a passionate gamer and model-maker who wrote his first wargame at the age of 15. He lives in the inexplicably named village of Old Wives Lees in Kent with his wife, a library of games, and a menagerie of beasts.

ILLUSTRATOR
David Auden Nash was born in Indiana, USA. He graduated with a BFA from DAAP at University of Cincinnati, and has been working in the illustration and design since 2008. He works primarily on board, card, and role-playing games, as well as books and video games.

PHOTOGRAPHY
All photographs shown in this book are from the author's own collection unless otherwise specified.

CONTENTS

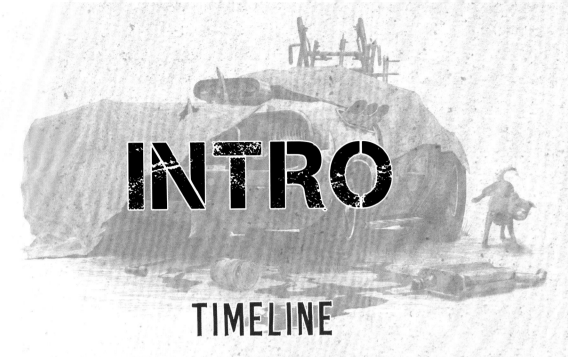

INTRO

TIMELINE

1969: *Apollo 11,* first manned Moon landing.
1976: *Ares 1,* first manned Mars landing.
1979: *August,* first Martian installation.
1982: Civilian Martian colonisation begins.
1991: Martian Secession.
1999: Martian Attack and Earth's collapse.
2008: Gaslands TV show launches.
2018: Present day. Gaslands 10-year anniversary.

GASLANDS

The year is 2018. Earth has been under Martian occupation for 19 years. The war left much of Earth destroyed and its population enslaved by the corporations of Mars and their relentless efficiency.

Earth is a ghetto. All money goes to Mars. While some resent those that betray their fellows to work for the Martian corporations, many simply cannot afford ideals.

The Internet is gone, but television continues under the global control of The Network: a nest of greedy and traitorous Martian collaborators. The Network's executive producer and chief anchor man, David Logan, is responsible for its line-up of ultra-violent blood sports and gas-guzzling death games.

The jewel in The Network's crown is Gaslands: broadcasting amateur and professional death races from across the world as teams battle for a place in the prime-time international final.

This spring Logan is offering a prize unique in the ten-year history of Gaslands. A one-way ticket to Mars. Escape from the broken and crumbling Earth to make a new life in that haven of the rich and happy.

The deadliest death races! The wildest half-time extravaganzas! The craziest audience participation! Everywhere David Logan's executive intervention can be felt. His vision is simple. This year must be the most spectacular Gaslands season yet.

Gaslands. Every Tuesday and Saturday night, 21:00 Central Mars Time.

WHAT IS GASLANDS?

This book contains a tabletop game that allows you to play cinematic, post-apocalyptic death sports with toy cars. To get your toy cars on the table, you need only read the basic and additional rules section of this book (see pages 14 and 38), and then try a run through of the "Street Race" introductory scenario (see page 62). You can then explore the rest of the book at your own pace; adding as many or as few additional options as you choose.

As well as being a tabletop game, *Gaslands* can also be an immersive hobby. Between games, you will find that many happy hours can be spent customising and painting your teams of toy cars, building scenery to race around, and generally bring to life the world in which your games take place. Take a look at the photos throughout this book for inspiration for what you can create with a little enthusiasm and ingenuity.

GASLANDS IN 60 SECONDS

Gaslands is a car combat game that combines toy cars, movement templates, and dice to allow you to race, skid, and blast your way through a post-apocalyptic dystopian future.

Here is how the game works in a nutshell:

Each round in *Gaslands* is split into six Gear Phases, and each vehicle can be in one of six Gears. Each round, you count up from Gear 1 to Gear 6 and in each Gear Phase you activate every vehicle currently in that Gear or higher. This means that cars in higher gears get to activate more than cars in lower Gears, so driving fast is good.

However, the faster you go, the fewer movement templates are available for you to select from. In particular, making sharper turns becomes difficult or impossible. Driving fast is good because you get more activations but you need to be careful, as you might not have the manoeuvrability to avoid that concrete wall you are speeding towards!

PEDAL TO THE METAL

When it is your turn to activate you check the Gear Phase number and then pick one of your vehicles that is in that Gear or higher which hasn't activated yet. You then pick a movement template. You can only choose from the templates with the correct "current Gear" shaded on them. It you are currently in Gear 2, for example, you can only choose templates with the "2" box shaded. If you pick up a template, you must use it. Don't pick up a template that you aren't allowed to use! If you do, someone else will get to pick and place your template instead, and they will probably drive you straight into that wall you were so keen to avoid.

Once you have picked your template, you place it down in front of your vehicle and then roll some Skid Dice. You can roll a number of Skid Dice up to your Handling Value, and they are the way that you will change up and down Gears, as well as how you perform cool manoeuvres like slides and spins. You don't have to roll any, and sometimes rolling none of them is the right choice.

THINGS WILL GET HAZARDOUS

The most common result on a Skid Die is a Shift, which allows you to change Gear up or down by one, but you pick up a Hazard Token. You also get Hazard Tokens for performing Hazardous manoeuvres (typically sharper turns in higher Gears), using Slide or Spin results on your Skid Dice, or for crashing into things.

These Hazard Tokens will start to build up quickly, so you need to keep an eye on them. If you have six Hazard Tokens at the end of *anyone's* activation, you Wipeout. Wiping out is bad for a few reasons. Firstly, you will drop to Gear

1, meaning you are unlikely to get any more activations this round, plus you might flip your vehicle, and then the player to your left gets to Spin your vehicle on the spot to face any direction they choose, likely into a barricade or straight off the table.

The Skid Dice are the key to keeping your Hazard Tokens under control. In addition to using them to change Gear, you can also use the Shift results to cancel out other Skid Dice that you don't want and also to clear Hazard Tokens from your vehicle's dashboard.

EXECUTIVE SUMMARY

On your turn in *Gaslands* you pick your template, roll your Skid Dice, move to the end of the template, and then make your shooting attacks. If you are getting shot at, you can try to evade the attacks. If you crash into anything, there are rules to cover that. Collisions are normally bad news for the lighter vehicle, and worse for everyone if they are head-on. Pick up too many Hazard Tokens and you Wipeout. Take too much damage and you get Wrecked (and might also explode). If you are racing, you must drive through the Gates, in order, in the right direction, and faster than the other guys. Have fun!

WHAT YOU'LL NEED

To play *Gaslands*, you'll need to gather the following:

TOY CARS

You'll need a small collection of post-apocalyptic cars, trucks or buggies in any scale. The rules assume you are using regular die-cast toy cars (roughly 20mm or 1/72 scale) which are inexpensive and readily available. There is no need to customise or paint your toy cars, but it will make things look a lot more awesome if you do!

DICE

You will need a dozen or so six-sided dice (D6) to play *Gaslands*.

MOVEMENT TEMPLATES

You will need a set of *Gaslands* movement templates to measure movement and shooting. You can photocopy these from the back of this book (or download them from Gaslands.com), stick them to some cereal box cardboard, and cut them out with scissors or a craft knife. You will also find links from the *Gaslands* website to many great companies who offer hard-wearing laser-cut template sets to improve your *Gaslands* games.

SKID DICE

Skid Dice are six-sided dice, with custom faces on them. If you do not have any Skid Dice, you can use normal D6 instead, by using the table below:

SKID DICE TABLE		
D6	Icon	Result
1	⚠	Hazard: Gain 1 Hazard Token.
2	SPIN	Spin: pivot up to 90 degrees in either direction. +1 Hazard Token
3	SLIDE	Slide: Slide as indicated by the Slide Exit Point on your movement template. +1 Hazard Token
4–6	SHIFT	Shift: cancel another result, change Gear up or down, or remove a Hazard Token.

If you are feeling industrious, you might want to make some custom Skid Dice, perhaps by printing the symbols on sticky labels and using blank dice. If you would rather use some purpose-made Skid Dice, check out the *Gaslands* website.

DASHBOARD CARDS

You will need one dashboard card for each vehicle you control. They are a quick reference for your vehicle and are used for recording current values for Hull Points and Gear. You can photocopy them from the back of this book or download them from the *Gaslands* website. Place a six-sided die (D6) in the gearbox, which is the box containing the max Gear Value, to keep track of your current Gear.

TABLE

You'll need a flat surface to play on. The specific size isn't too important. *Gaslands* works great on most sizes of table.

TERRAIN

Custom scenery, such as: obstacles, areas of rough ground, tin shacks, barricades, ramps, oil cans, or road sections, will add much to the game, but are not required. You can drive around salt and pepper shakers if needs be.

TOKENS

At a minimum, you will need a set of tokens to represent Hazard Tokens. Gaming gems, bottle caps, nuts and bolts, or tokens scavenged from other board games (in true post-apocalyptic style!) all work great.

You may also find it convenient to use tokens to track which vehicle has activated, how much ammo weapons have left, who has Pole Position, and so on, but this is not required. You will find a full selection of tokens and markers at the rear of this book.

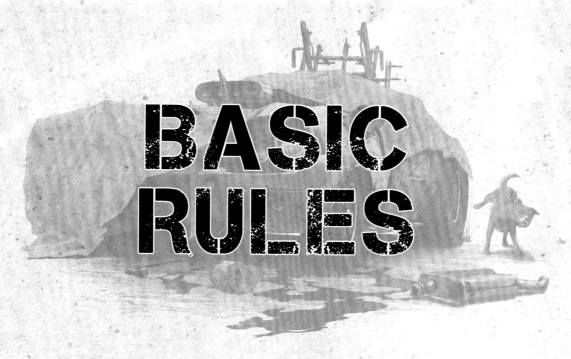

BASIC RULES

This Basic Rules section lays out the basic shape of the game. In combination with the Additional Rules section (see page 38), these form the core rules of *Gaslands*. Read both and you will be ready to play your first game of *Gaslands*. Once you are comfortable with the core rules in these two sections, you can explore the Creating a Team, Advanced Rules, and Ways to Play sections to find additional options to expand your games (see pages 63, 68 and 122).

THE BASICS

THE RULE OF CARNAGE

In *Gaslands*, if a rule is unclear, choose whichever option results in the most carnage for all concerned. This is **The Rule of Carnage**.

SPECIFIC RULES

The text of a specific rule can conflict with the general rules. In case of a conflict, the text relating to the more specific circumstance overrides the more general rule.

SIMULTANEOUS EFFECTS

If the effects of multiple special rules occur at the same time, the controller of the active vehicle decides the order of resolution.

VEHICLES

The vehicles are the stars of *Gaslands*. Vehicles are defined by the following statistics:

NAME

Give your vehicle or driver a badass name, so the crowds know who to root for.

MAX GEAR

Every vehicle has a Maximum Gear Value. A vehicle's current Gear may never exceed its Max Gear. See Movement (page 21).

HANDLING

Every vehicle has a Handling Value, which affects how many Skid Dice the vehicle can roll. See Skid Dice (page 12).

CREW

Every vehicle has a Crew Value, which indicates how many attacks a vehicle can make during its Attack Step. See Attack Step (page 30). Every crewmember is armed with a Handgun by default.

WEIGHT

Every vehicle has a Weight, which indicates how solid and heavy it is. For example, bikes are Lightweight, cars are Middleweight, and buses are Heavyweight. See Collisions (page 52) and Explosions (page 44).

HULL

A vehicle's Hull Value indicates how much punishment it can take before it is immobilised (perhaps in a ball of flames). A vehicle begins the game with a number of Hull Points equal to its Hull Value. Hull Points are reduced by enemy attacks and Collisions. When a vehicle is reduced to zero Hull Points it is Wrecked. See Damage (page 43).

CURRENT GEAR

Each vehicle has a current Gear Value between 1 and 6. Place a six-sided dice (D6) in the gearbox on the vehicle's dashboard card, with the appropriate side face-up to show the vehicle's current Gear. A vehicle's current Gear may never exceed its Max Gear.

All vehicles start the game in Gear 1. Do not "reset" a vehicle's current Gear from round to round, all vehicles begin each round in the Gear that they ended the previous round in.

HAZARD TOKENS

Vehicles gain Hazard Tokens when they change gear, spin, slide, and from other effects. When a vehicle gains a Hazard Token, place it on the vehicle's dashboard. As you will see later on, if a vehicle ever has 6 or more Hazard Tokens at the start of *any* player's Wipeout step, that vehicle will Wipeout. See Wipeout Step, (page 34).

Hazard Tokens can be removed using Shift results, as you'll see in Skid Dice (page 12).

If you are playing with Audience Votes, you can also use Thunderous Applause to remove Hazard Tokens (See page 89).

MOVEMENT TEMPLATES

There are nine movement templates that players may select from when moving their vehicle. These are Gentle, Turn, Hard, Hairpin, Veer, Swerve, and three lengths of straight: Short Straight, Medium Straight, and Long Straight.

Movement templates may be placed either way up. The three straight templates must always be placed with the Slide Exit Point at the far end of the movement template, away from the vehicle. The other movement templates may be placed with either of their short ends touching the vehicle.

PERMITTED GEARS

Each movement template has a set of icons that indicate the gears in which that movement template is permitted. The permitted Gears are the shaded Gear numbers on the movement template.

TRIVIAL AND HAZARDOUS MANOEUVRES

The icons directly below the shaded Gear on the template indicate whether the movement template is Trivial or Hazardous for a vehicle currently in that gear. See Trivial Manoeuvres (page 40) and Hazardous Manoeuvres (page 48).

SLIDE EXIT POINT

Each template also has a notched arrow, which indicates the Slide Exit Position (see page 24).

TEMPLATE SUMMARY

Here's a quick reference of which Gears each template is permitted in, and in which Gears each is either Hazardous or Trivial:

TEMPLATE SUMMARY TABLE						
Gear	1	2	3	4	5	6
Short Straight	SHIFT					
Medium Straight	SHIFT	SHIFT	SHIFT	SHIFT		
Long Straight						
Gentle	SHIFT	SHIFT		⚠		
Turn	SHIFT			⚠		
Hard	SHIFT		⚠			
Hairpin			⚠			
Veer		SHIFT		⚠		
Swerve				⚠	⚠	

THE ROUND
ROUND STRUCTURE

A game of *Gaslands* is played in rounds. Each round is then divided into 6 Gear Phases, from 1 to 6.

In each Gear Phase, starting with the player with Pole Position, players alternate the activation of qualifying vehicles, until all qualifying vehicles have activated in that Gear Phase.

When a vehicle activates, it will first move in the Movement Step, then potentially attack in the Attack Step, and then *any* vehicle with too many Hazard Tokens will Wipeout in the Wipeout Step.

Once there are no more qualifying vehicles to activate in a Gear Phase, play proceeds to the next Gear Phase, beginning again with the player in Pole Position. This sequence repeats until all vehicles have activated in every applicable Gear Phase, then the round ends and a new round begins with Gear Phase 1.

Players continue to play rounds in this manner until the game end condition, which is determined by the scenario, is met.

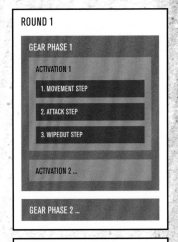

ROUND 1

GEAR PHASE 1

ACTIVATION 1

1. MOVEMENT STEP

2. ATTACK STEP

3. WIPEOUT STEP

ACTIVATION 2 ...

GEAR PHASE 2 ...

ROUND 2 ...

GEAR PHASES

Each round is split into six Gear Phases, resolved in ascending order (i.e. starting with Gear Phase 1 and ending with Gear Phase 6).

In each Gear Phase, beginning with the player in Pole Position and proceeding clockwise, players take turns activating a single qualifying vehicle, and **must** activate a qualifying vehicle if they have one.

When it is their turn to activate a vehicle, if a player has more than one vehicle that currently qualifies for an activation, that player may choose any of their qualifying vehicles to activate.

When it is their turn to activate a vehicle, if a player has no qualifying vehicles, they must pass. When a player passes, they do not activate a vehicle, and play passes clockwise to the next player. A player who still has qualifying vehicles cannot pass.

Once all players have passed consecutively, this Gear Phase ends and the next begins.

If you are playing with Audience Votes, you get a chance to spend votes before you are forced to pass, allowing you the possibility of getting back into the game. *See page 88 for more information.*

QUALIFYING FOR AN ACTIVATION

To qualify for an activation in a given Gear Phase the vehicle's current Gear must be equal to or greater than the Gear Phase number, and it must not have activated in this Gear Phase.

A qualifying vehicle cannot pass, it must activate.

For example: a car in Gear 2 will activate in the first two Gear Phases, and not in the remaining four (assuming it does not change gear during its activation); a motorbike in Gear 6 will activate in all six Gear Phases.

Players check whether a vehicle qualifies for an activation at the point at which the player has an opportunity to activate a vehicle, (not at the start of the round or the Gear Phase). In this way, changing Gear in an earlier Gear Phase will allow the vehicle to activate in a later one. Similarly, suffering a Wipeout before getting a chance to activate can causes a vehicle to miss its activation later in the Gear Phase.

POLE POSITION

The player in Pole Position must activate the first vehicle in each Gear Phase.

The scenario determines which player starts with Pole Position, and when Pole Position passes from player to player.

ACTIVATIONS

When a player has an opportunity to activate a vehicle, they must first declare the qualifying vehicle that they wish to activate, and then perform the following steps with that vehicle, in order:

1. **Movement Step:** in which the player selects and places a movement template, rolls some Skid Dice, and then moves their vehicle into its Final Position.
2. **Attack Step:** in which the player declares targets and makes attacks
3. **Wipeout Step:** in which all players check if any vehicle they control has 6 Hazard Tokens, and every vehicle that does suffers a Wipeout.

During a vehicle's activation, it is referred to as the "active vehicle".

MOVEMENT STEP

In the Movement Step, you select and place a movement template. Then you have the chance to roll some Skid Dice, and then you move your vehicle into its Final Position, which normally means placing the vehicle at the far end of the movement template or slide template.

MOVEMENT STEP TIMING

During a vehicle's Movement Step, follow this sequence:

1.1.   **Select** a movement template.
1.2.   **Place** the movement template.
1.3.   **Roll Skid Dice**, up to the Handling Value of the vehicle.
1.4.   **Spend Shift results**:
  • Discard one Hazard Slide or Spin result.
  • Change Gear up or down by 1, +1 Hazard Token.
  • Discard one Hazard Token from this vehicle.
  • Discard without effect.
1.5.   **Gain Hazard Tokens** from uncancelled Hazard, Slide, and Spin results.
1.6.   **Place Slide template** if the vehicle had an uncancelled Slide result.
1.7.   **Move** the vehicle into its **Final Position.**
COLLISION WINDOW
1.8.   **Spin** the vehicle if the vehicle had an uncancelled Spin result.
COLLISION WINDOW

Important! The vehicle does not actually "move" until Step 1.7, and therefore does not trigger a Collision until that point.

SELECTING A MOVEMENT TEMPLATE

At the start of a vehicle's Movement Step, its controller must select a single permitted movement template.

A permitted movement template is one which has the current Gear of the vehicle listed as one of its permitted Gears.

For example: any vehicle that is currently in Gear 2, 3, or 4 may select the Veer movement template. This movement template is not permitted for vehicles that are in Gear 5, who must select one of the Gentle, Swerve, or Long Straight movement templates.

Players may not "pre-measure" their next movement during their, or another player's, activation.

PLACING THE MOVEMENT TEMPLATE

After selecting a template, the player places it with either of the short edges of the template parallel with, and centred on, the front edge of the vehicle. Do not move the vehicle along the template yet. The player first has the option to roll some Skid Dice.

SKID DICE

After selecting and placing their movement template, the active player declares and rolls a number of Skid Dice up to the Handling Value of the active vehicle. A player may choose to declare to roll no Skid Dice. All declared Skid Dice must be rolled at once.

RESOLVING SKID DICE

Once rolled, all Skid Dice results must be resolved. You can spend Shift results for various effects, and any uncancelled Spins or Slides will affect your vehicle's Final Position.

To resolve the effects of the Skid Dice, check the timing chart above, and be sure to apply the results in the correct order. First, spend your Shift results, then gain Hazard Tokens from uncancelled Hazard, Slide and Spin results. Then place the Slide template if the vehicle had an uncancelled Slide result. Then move into your Final Position. Finally, Spin the vehicle if the vehicle had an uncancelled Spin result.

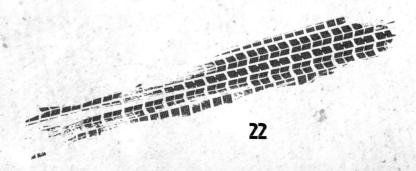

SHIFT

Shift results must be resolved first. Each Shift result is resolved one at a time and may be used for any of the following effects, in any order. "Spend" means to discard for an effect.

Spend any number of Shift results to cancel one Spin, Slide or Hazard result for each Shift result spent. Cancelled results are discarded.

Spend any number of Shift results to immediately discard a Hazard Token from the vehicle for each Shift result spent.

Spend any number of Shift results to immediately change Gear up or down once for each Shift result spent, gaining 1 Hazard Token each time.

Unspent Shift results may be discarded for no effect.

CHANGING GEAR

Whenever a vehicle changes Gear, the vehicle immediately gains a Hazard Token (unless otherwise noted). A vehicle may change Gear any number of times in a single activation, gaining a Hazard Token each time. Normally, a vehicle will change Gear through the use of Shift results on the Skid Dice and Trivial manoeuvres, but other effects can also result in a vehicle changing Gear.

If you are playing with Audience Votes, you can use "Burn Rubber" to change Gear. See page 89 for more information.

GAIN HAZARDS

After resolving all Shift results, the active vehicle gains 1 Hazard Token for each un-cancelled Hazard, Slide, or Spin result.

Because all Shift results must be spent before gaining other Hazards, you cannot avoid gaining the Hazard from a Slide or Spin result if you choose to resolve it. You'll have to remove it in a later Movement Step.

SLIDE

If the vehicle has one or more un-cancelled Slide results, take the Slide template and place it adjacent to the Slide Exit Point on the movement template. The protruding arrow on the Slide template should be inserted into the matching "notch" in the movement template. The Slide result changes the location of the Final Position of the movement. See Final Position, page 25.

If a vehicle has multiple un-cancelled Slide results, the vehicle doesn't place additional Slide templates, but does gain additional Hazard Tokens in Step 1.5.

SPIN

If the vehicle has one or more un-cancelled Spin results, and the vehicle hasn't ended its move in an Interrupted Final Position (see Interrupted Movement page 45), the vehicle may be pivot up to 90 degrees in either direction about its centre point.

This pivot can a cause Collision, if the pivot brings the vehicle into contact with an obstruction it didn't start the pivot in contact with. (See Collisions, page 52).

If a Collision causes the vehicle to end its movement in an Interrupted Final Position (see page 46), the vehicle does not get to Spin, but still gains the Hazard Token.

It is perfectly legal to Spin a vehicle "zero degrees", but the vehicle must still take the Hazard Token from the Spin result. Multiple spin results do not permit a vehicle to be rotated any further, but they do add additional Hazard Tokens.

SKID DICE TACTICS

At first glance, it will look like the Skid Dice have some "good" results and some "bad" results. While it is often true that you don't want to roll Slides and Spins, sometimes those are just the results you want to pull off an amazing Slide around an obstacle, line yourself up for your next move, or to get a bead on someone with your guns. Look for opportunities to use these Skid Dice results in your favour and the crowd will go wild.

FINAL POSITION
MOVING INTO FINAL POSITION

To move a vehicle from its starting position to its Final Position. Pick the vehicle up and place it at the far end of the movement template such that the rear edge of the vehicle is parallel with the far end of the template, and the rear edge of the vehicle is centred on the far end of the template.

If anything is overlapping either the vehicle's movement template or its Final Position, check the Interrupted Movement rules on page 45 to find out what happens.

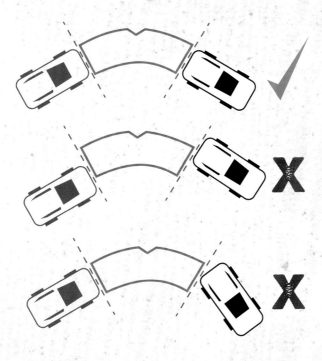

SLIDING INTO FINAL POSITION

If the vehicle resolved a Slide result during this Movement Step, it must be placed with the side edge of the vehicle that was furthest from the Slide template parallel with the far end of the Slide template, such that the side edge of the vehicle is centred on the far end of the Slide template.

If the slide is coming off a straight template, the player controlling the active vehicle may choose which direction to face the vehicle in.

WEAPONS

Weapons in *Gaslands* are defined by the following statistics:

- **Range**: This determines which shooting template this weapon uses to measure range.
- **Facing**: This determines the arc of fire of this weapon.
- **Attack dice**: This determines the number of dice this weapons rolls when it attacks.

SHOOTING TEMPLATES

There are six sizes of shooting template:

- Short Range.
- Medium Range.
- Long Range.
- Double Range.
- Large Burst.
- Small Burst.

SHORT, MEDIUM, AND LONG RANGE

The Short, Medium, and Long range shooting templates are identical to the Short, Medium and Long Straight movement templates respectively. Use the matching movement template whenever those shooting templates are required.

DOUBLE RANGE

The Double range shooting template is constructed by placing the short edges of the Medium Straight and Long Straight movement templates end-to-end to form a single linear template, as shown below:

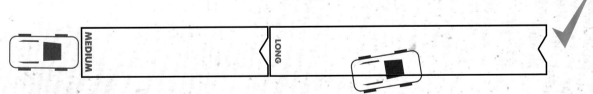

Front-mounted Double Range

BURST TEMPLATES

There are two sizes of burst template: the Large Burst template and the Small Burst template. These are specific shaped templates that can be found in the back of this book.

Side-mounted Large Burst

RANGE

Shooting ranges are measured using the shooting template. Place the shooting template within the weapon's Arc of Fire and measure the two closest points between the attacker and the target. If any part of the shooting template can touch the target, it may be attacked.

ARC OF FIRE AND FACING

When arming a vehicle with a weapon, the player must declare a single facing for that weapon. A weapon's facing determines the weapon's Arc of Fire.

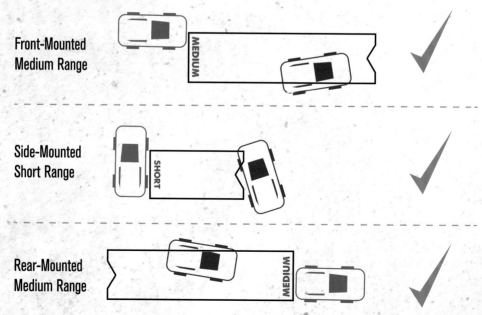

Front-Mounted Medium Range

Side-Mounted Short Range

Rear-Mounted Medium Range

FRONT-MOUNTED

A weapon that is front-mounted has a Front Arc of Fire. To check if a target is in a vehicle's Front Arc of Fire, place the shooting template such that its short edge is touching any part of the front edge of the vehicle, exactly parallel to the vehicle's side edge, and extending forward from the front edge of the vehicle. The template may be placed anywhere along the front edge of the vehicle, but must be exactly parallel.

REAR-MOUNTED

A weapon that is rear-mounted has a Rear Arc of Fire. To check if a target is in a vehicle's Rear Arc of Fire, place the shooting template such that its short edge is touching any part of the rear of the vehicle and extending backwards from the rear of the vehicle. The template may be placed anywhere along the rear edge of the vehicle, but must be exactly parallel.

SIDE-MOUNTED

A weapon that is side-mounted has a Side Arc of Fire. To check if a target is in either of a vehicle's Side Arcs of Fire, place the shooting template such that its short edge is touching any part of either of the side edges of the vehicle, exactly perpendicular to the vehicle's side edge, and extending out from the side edge of the vehicle. The template may be placed anywhere along the edge of the vehicle, as long as it is touching the side of the vehicle and is exactly perpendicular to its side edge.

360-DEGREE ARC OF FIRE

Turret-mounted weapons, and those that are crew fired (such as Handguns, Grenades, and Molotov Cocktails) have a 360-degree Arc of Fire. Other weapons may have a 360-degree arc of fire if listed as such.

If a weapon has a 360-degree Arc of Fire then the shooting template may be placed such that its short edge is touching any part of the vehicle and facing in any direction.

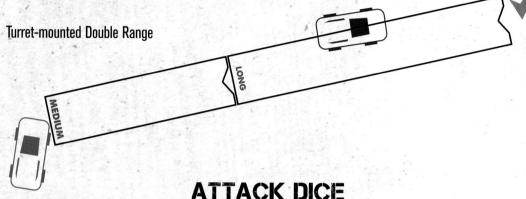

Turret-mounted Double Range

ATTACK DICE

Each weapon has an attack dice value. This is the number of D6s that the vehicle rolls when making an attack with this weapon.

ATTACK STEP

During a vehicle's Attack Step, follow this sequence:

2.1 Declare targets and check range.
2.2 **Roll Attack Dice:** 4+ to hit, 6 is critical (2 hits).
COLLISION WINDOW
2.3 **Evade:** Each 6+ cancels one hit.
2.4 **Damage:** Remove Hull Points.

DECLARE TARGETS

The player must declare a single target for each weapon it is attacking with. Targets must be within range and arc or fire of that weapon.

Only other vehicles are valid targets, unless the scenario specifies otherwise. A vehicle may target friendly or enemy vehicles.

Each weapon may select a target independently; a vehicle is not forced to fire all its weapons at a single target.

PRE-MEASURING

Players may measure shooting ranges before declaring targets.

NUMBER OF ATTACKS

During its Attack Step, a vehicle may attack any number of times up to the Crew Value of the vehicle. Each weapon a vehicle is armed with may only be selected to attack once during a single Attack Step.

If a vehicle is armed with several copies of a single weapon (for example, two Miniguns), it may attack once with each of those copies, as long as the number of attacks does not exceed the Crew Value of the vehicle.

HANDGUNS

Regardless of any weapons that a vehicle has been specifically armed with, every vehicle counts as being armed with an unlimited number of Handguns. Handguns are "crew fired" and so benefit from a 360-degree Arc of Fire.

ROLL ATTACK DICE

To make an attack, roll a number of D6 equal to the weapon's attack dice value. For each roll of a 4+, the target suffers a hit. When attacking a single target with multiple weapons, roll all the attack dice at the same time.

ROLL EVADE DICE

After the attacker has rolled **all** their attack dice for this Attack Step against a single target and calculated the total number of hits the target is suffering, the target may make a single Evade attempt.

To Evade, the target vehicle's controller rolls a number of Evade dice equal to the vehicle's current Gear. Each roll of a 6+ on an Evade die cancels one hit.

You don't Evade each weapon separately. Wait until the attacker has rolled the attack dice from all their weapons, and then make your Evade roll against the combined hits.

SUFFER DAMAGE

After Evading, each un-cancelled hit causes the target to suffer one point of damage, which removes 1 Hull Point. Record this by marking off lost Hull Points on the vehicle's dashboard. When a vehicle has lost all of its Hull Points, it gets Wrecked. See Damage, page 43.

WIPEOUT STEP

Any vehicle with 6 or more Hazard Tokens during the Wipeout Step suffers a Wipeout, regardless of whose Wipeout Step it is.

The Wipeout Step is the final step in a vehicle's activation, but it can affect any vehicle, not just the active vehicle.

If more than one vehicle needs to resolve a Wipeout in the same Wipeout Step, resolve the active vehicle's Wipeout first, and then resolve the remaining Wipeouts in clockwise order of their controllers.

Generally, vehicles will Wipeout because they started the step with 6 or more Hazard Tokens, but it's also possible for Collisions and other carnage to result in a vehicle gaining enough Hazard Tokens during this step to Wipeout as well.

WIPEOUT

If a vehicle suffers a Wipeout, perform the following steps:

3.1 **Flip check:** If lower than current Gear, suffer 2 hits and forced move Medium Straight forward
COLLISION WINDOW
3.2 **Reset:** Regardless of the Flip check, reduce current Gear to 1 and discard all Hazard Tokens from the vehicle
3.3 **Lose Control:** Regardless of flip check, the player clockwise of the player controlling the active vehicle pivots the vehicle about its centre point to any facing.
COLLISION WINDOW

FLIP CHECK

When a vehicle suffers a Wipeout, it must first make a Flip check to see if it Flips.
To make a Flip check, the player controlling the vehicle rolls a D6. If the roll is equal to or higher than the vehicle's current Gear, all is fine. If the roll is lower than the vehicle's current Gear: the vehicle immediately suffers a flip.
For example, if a vehicle is in Gear 5, a 5+ is needed to avoid a flip.

RESET CURRENT GEAR AND HAZARD TOKENS

Regardless of the result of the Flip check, the vehicle that has suffered the Wipeout must then reduce its current Gear to 1 and discard all Hazard Tokens.

LOSE CONTROL

In the final step in the Wipeout, the player clockwise of the vehicle's controller pivots the vehicle about its centre point to any facing. This pivot can cause a Collision, if the pivot brings the vehicle into contact with an obstruction it didn't start the pivot in contact with. (See Collisions, page 52).

Wipeouts might seem pretty crippling at first, but if you are playing with Audience Votes, you might be able to use "Burn Rubber" to get back into the game, as well as using "Thunderous Applause" to better avoid a Wipeout in the first place. See page 88 for more information.

FLIP

When a vehicle suffers a Flip, that vehicle suffers 2 hits, and then makes a forced move medium straight directly forward, ignoring all obstructions, including other vehicles. This movement causes a Collision Window. The damage from a Flip cannot be evaded.

EXAMPLE ACTIVATION

Its is Gear Phase 2. The Blue car is currently in Gear 2. It is heading towards a big rock, so the Blue player eyeballs the situation and decides the Turn template should be enough to get her around the boulder. Placing it in front of the car, it turns out she just misjudged it. The rock ever so slightly overlaps with Blue's Final Position. She doesn't want to hit the obstacle, so before moving into her Final Position, Blue decides to pick up some Skid Dice. She declares she is rolling all three Skid Dice permitted by her handling of 3.

The Skid Dice roll two Shifts and a Slide. The slide is just what Blue needs to dodge the rock, so she decides not to cancel that result with one of her Shifts. Instead, she spends the first Shift to change into Gear 3, to ensure she gets another activation next Gear Phase, and spends the second Shift to discard the Hazard Token she just gained for changing Gear.

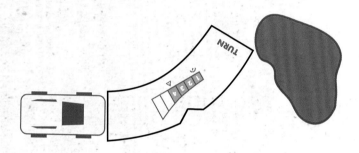

Blue can't avoid picking up a Hazard Token for the slide she wants to resolve, so she puts that on her car's dashboard and then places the Slide template into the matching notch on the turn template. She picks up her car and places it down in her Final Position at the end of the Slide template, making sure she has the vehicle facing in the right direction. Blue doesn't have anyone to shoot at and only has 1 Hazard Token, so doesn't Wipeout. Play passes to the next player.

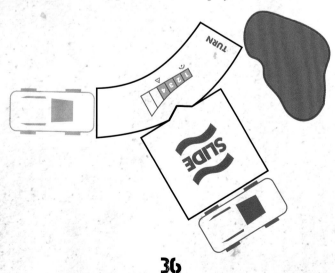

ADDITIONAL RULES

You should now be familiar with the basics of *Gaslands*; how to Move, Shoot, and Wipeout. This section contains additional rules to deal with other situations you will encounter, including Collisions, as well as adding a bit more detail to the Movement and Attack Steps. The basic rules plus the additional rules form the core rules of *Gaslands*.

ADDITIONAL MOVEMENT RULES

HAZARDOUS MANOEUVRES

If there is a hazard icon directly below the shaded Gear for the active vehicle's current Gear on the selected movement template, this manoeuvre is Hazardous.

When a vehicle's controller selects a Hazardous manoeuvre, the vehicle immediately gains a Hazard Token.

For example, the Veer template is Hazardous if you are in Gear 4. If you select the Veer movement while in Gear 4, the vehicle immediately gains a Hazard Token.

THE "TOUCH IT, USE IT" RULE

Once a player has touched a movement template during step 1.1 of their Movement Step, they **must** then select that movement template. They may not pick up a template and then put in down in favour of another template.

If a player selects a template that is not permitted, then the player to their left

38

must select and place any permitted template for this vehicle. The active vehicle may not roll any Skid Dice but must apply any free icons from a Hazardous or Trivial manoeuvre, and the resolution of these icons is controlled by the active player.

The Touch It, Use It rule exists to ensure that players choose their templates decisively and do not take overly long about testing endless template options to find the perfect one. This is a game about high-speed vehicular mayhem after all! You may (as with any rule in GASLANDS) choose to ignore this rule if all players agree.

REVERSING

If a vehicle is in Gear 1, it may move in Reverse. To move in Reverse, the player controlling the active vehicle selects any template permitted in Gear 1 and uses it to move backwards. Place the template as normal, except it is placed with its short edge parallel with and centred on the **rear** edge of the vehicle, rather than the front. A vehicle moving in Reverse may roll Skid Dice and change Gear as normal.

REVERSING INTO FINAL POSITION

If the player chose to move the active vehicle in Reverse during this Movement Step, the vehicle's Final Position is such that the front edge of the vehicle is touching the far edge of the movement template.

FORCED MOVE

Some game effects, for example suffering a Flip or being Wrecked, can result in a vehicle being forced to move, sometimes even outside of their Movement Step. When a vehicle is forced to move, the vehicle first selects and places the indicated movement template, and then moves into Final Position (see Final Position page 25) as an interruption to the normal course of play, before returning to the normal activation sequence.

During a forced move, no Skid Dice are rolled, the permitted Gear icons are ignored on the template, and the movement counts as neither Trivial nor Hazardous. A forced move always causes a Collision Window to occur (see Collisions, page 52).

ADDITIONAL SKID DICE RULES

TRIVIAL MANOEUVRES

If there is a Shift icon directly below the shaded Gear for the active vehicle's current Gear on the movement template, this manoeuvre is Trivial.

When a vehicle's controller selects a trivial manoeuvre, the vehicle gains a bonus Shift result during this Movement Step, as if the player had rolled an additional Skid Dice and got a Shift.

PUSH IT

After rolling the Skid Dice, the player may choose to Push It. If a player chooses to Push It, he or she may add 1 Hazard Token to the vehicle to pick up any number of the rolled Skid Dice and reroll them.

When choosing to Push It, the player does not have to reroll all of their Skid Dice, they can keep some results as they are and reroll others.

A player may only push it once during any Movement Step.

YOUR FIRST ACTIVATION

You'll find out soon enough that Hazards and Wipeouts are a fact of life in Gaslands. However, you really don't want to Wipeout on your first activation!

If this is your first game of Gaslands, we strongly recommend you select the Medium Straight on your first activation and avoid rolling any Skid Dice. The medium straight template is trivial in Gear 1, and so you can use its free Shift to change into Gear 2 (gaining a Hazard Token). This guarantees you are going to get another activation in Gear Phase 2, even if you get collided with a couple of time.

In Gear Phase 2, you will be able shift up again to ensure you activate in Gear Phase 3. It might be tempting to roll some Skid Dice on your first activation of a game, but leave those tricksy little cubes for Gear Phase 2.

SKID DICE EXAMPLE ONE

A car, with Handling 3, is in current Gear 2 and has no Hazard Tokens. The player selects a Medium Straight movement, which is Trivial in current Gear 2, places it and rolls three Skid Dice. The dice roll a Slide and two Shifts. The player adds another Shift from the Trivial manoeuvre , for three Shifts in total. The player uses the first Shift result to change up into current Gear 3, adding a Hazard Token to the vehicle. The player uses the second Shift to remove that Hazard Token, and then uses the third Shift result to cancel and discard the Slide result. As the Slide result has been cancelled, it provides no Hazard Token. The car is now in Gear 3 and ends with no Hazard Tokens.

SKID DICE EXAMPLE TWO

A truck, with Handling 2, is in current Gear 3 and has 4 Hazard Tokens at the start of its activation. The player selects a Hard movement, which is Hazardous in Gear 3, and immediately gains the penalty hazard result from selecting a Hazardous movement, bring it to 5 Hazard Tokens. The player then (unwisely) decides to roll 2 Skid Dice. One die rolls a Slide and the other rolls a Hazard. These dice currently are going to cause the pickup truck to gain two Hazard Tokens, bringing it to a total of 7 and a Wipeout. The player decides to take a risk, and places a sixth Hazard Token on the pickup truck's dashboard to Push It, hoping to roll a pair of Shifts.

The player rerolls both Skid Dice and, happily, both roll Shift results. The player uses both of the Shift results to remove Hazard Tokens from the truck's dashboard. The truck ends this Skid Dice resolution in Gear 3 and back on 4 Hazard Tokens, meaning it is safe when the Wipeout Step arrives.

ADDITIONAL ATTACK RULES

DISTRACTED

If the active vehicle is touching an obstruction at the start of its Attack Step, the active vehicle is Distracted and cannot make any shooting attacks or dropped weapon attacks.

COVER

If the shooting template overlaps an obstruction **before** it touches the target, the target benefits from Cover. When shooting a target benefits from Cover, the attacker suffers a -1 penalty to hit on their attack dice, normally therefore requiring a 5+ to hit. Critical Hits still occur on the natural roll of a 6.

CRITICAL HITS

Each natural 6 rolled on an attack dice counts as a Critical Hit and causes the target to suffer one additional hit. This additional hit counts as a normal hit from the same weapon.

Critical Hits cause two separate hits, which need to be evaded separately.

EVADING SPECIAL ATTACKS

Some weapons have special rules, for example Blast, that trigger only if the weapon damages the target. When rolling to Evade, always cancel hits that **do not** trigger special rules first, and then only cancel hits that trigger special rules after all standard hits have all been cancelled. If there are hits that trigger different special rules, the controller of the target vehicle decides in which order the hits are cancelled.

DAMAGE

HULL POINTS

When a vehicle suffers damage, for each point of damage received it removes 1 Hull Point. Record this by marking off lost Hull Points on the vehicle's dashboard.

GETTING WRECKED

When a vehicle has lost all its Hull Points, it gets Wrecked.
When a vehicle gets Wrecked, follow these steps:

1   **Skid to A Halt:** Forced move Short Straight forward.
COLLISION WINDOW
2   **Reset:** Reduce current Gear to 1 and discard all Hazard Tokens from the vehicle.
3   **Explosion Check:** Roll D6 + ammo tokens, explodes on 6+.
4   **Get Wrecked:** Turn model over, leave in play as a wreck.

Losing a vehicle doesn't have to be permanent in Gaslands. If you are playing with Audience Votes, you can use them to respawn your last vehicle and keep in the game. See page 88 for more information.

SKID TO A HALT

If a vehicle gets Wrecked, it skids to a halt. Immediately make a forced move Short Straight directly forward with the vehicle.

RESET CURRENT GEAR AND HAZARDS

After skidding to a halt, the vehicle reduces its current Gear to 1 and discards all Hazard Tokens.

EXPLOSION CHECK

After skidding to a halt and resetting its current Gear and Hazards, the vehicle must make an Explosion check. To make an Explosion check, roll a D6 and add the number of ammo tokens the vehicle is carrying. If the result is 6 or more, the vehicle immediately explodes (see page 44).

GET WRECKED

As the final step in the process of getting Wrecked, the vehicle's model is turned over onto its roof and it becomes a wreck. This wreck remains in play. As soon as a vehicle becomes a wreck, it ceases to be a vehicle.

TWISTED METAL

If a vehicle gets Wrecked during a Collision, perhaps due to damage from a Smash Attack, remove its wreck from play after resolving all the steps in the wrecking process.

If a vehicle that is getting Wrecked is involved in a Collision during skidding to a halt, remove it from play after resolving the all steps in the wrecking process.

When one of your vehicles is Wrecked you receive an Audience Vote. The audiences at home love a bit of carnage! See page 88 for Audience Votes.

EXPLOSIONS

When a vehicle Explodes, make an attack against each vehicle within Medium range of the exploding vehicle in a 360-degree Arc of Fire, and then remove the vehicle from play. Treat each as a separate attack with the Blast special rule (see page 81) and a number of attack dice determined by the weight of the exploding vehicle. Damage from explosions can be evaded.

VEHICLE EXPLOSION TABLE	
Weight	Explosion Attack Dice
Lightweight	2D6
Middleweight	4D6
Heavyweight	6D6

BLAST

For every un-cancelled hit caused by a weapon or effect with the Blast rule, the target immediately gains 1 Hazard Token.

WRECKS

A wreck is a destructible obstacle with a weight equal to the weight of the vehicle it was before it became a wreck.

If a vehicle collides with a wreck, remove the wreck from play immediately after resolving the Collision.

OBSTRUCTIONS

Vehicles, obstacles and wrecks all count as obstructions. If a movement template or a vehicle's final position overlaps an obstruction then a Collision will likely occur, unless the player can find a clever way to slide around the obstruction using their Skid Dice.

STARTING IN CONTACT WITH AN OBSTRUCTION

If a vehicle starts a Movement Step touching an obstruction, that vehicle must ignore the obstruction for that Movement Step.

INTERRUPTED MOVEMENT

If the selected movement template causes any part of the vehicle's movement template or Final Position to overlap with an obstruction that it is not ignoring, the vehicle's movement is interrupted.

The Interrupted Movement rules will seem a little involved on first reading but it's mostly common sense. The vehicle will end up as far down the template as it will go, stopping as soon as it collides with something.

INTERRUPTED FINAL POSITION

If a vehicle's movement is interrupted, an Interrupted Final Position must be found. This Interrupted Final Position overrides the normal Final Position.

To find the vehicle's Interrupted Final Position, move the active vehicle forward along the movement template from its starting position towards its Final Position until any part of the active vehicle touches an obstruction that it is not ignoring.

If the vehicle can be placed at this position such that it does not overlap any obstruction (even one that it is ignoring), then this becomes the vehicle's Interrupted Final Position. A vehicle's Interrupted Final Position will always leave the vehicle touching an obstruction.

Once the Interrupted Final Position is found, resolve a Collision with any obstruction the vehicle is touching (and not ignoring). If the obstruction was not removed as a result of the Collision, the active vehicle ends its movement in its Interrupted Final Position.

Remember that if a vehicle starts a Movement Step touching an obstruction, that vehicle must ignore the obstruction for that Movement Step.

FINDING THE INTERRUPTED FINAL POSITION

While moving the vehicle forwards along the template to find an Interrupted Final Position, ensure that the vehicle follows the line and is parallel to the direction of travel of the template to that point. Make sure the vehicle is centred on the template and is covering as much of the surface area of the movement template as possible.

MULTIPLE OBSTRUCTIONS

If the vehicle can't be placed in its Interrupted Final Position because another obstruction is in the way, continue to move the active vehicle backwards along the movement template until it is not overlapping any obstruction (even one that it is ignoring). This becomes the vehicle's Interrupted Final Position.

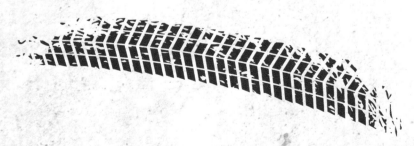

INTERRUPTED MOVEMENT EXAMPLE

In this example, the Blue car has selected and placed a turn template which overlaps the Red car. Blue is moved along its movement template until it comes into contact with Red. This becomes Blue's Interrupted Final Position, and Blue ends its movement there. As there is a Collision Window right after Movement Step 1.7, a Collision is immediately resolved.

WIDE VEHICLES

In some circumstances, a vehicle that is physically wider that the movement template can "squeeze" past a nearby obstruction, as long as no part of the vehicle's movement template or Final Position overlaps an obstruction. In other situations, the movement will be interrupted by some later obstruction and cause the wide vehicle to bump into a nearer obstruction that it otherwise would have "squeezed" past had it not been for the second obstruction causing the movement to count as interrupted. You'll just have to apply some cinematic imagination to explain the occasional edge case.

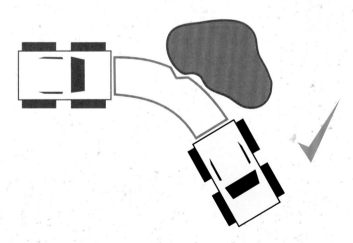

IGNORING OBSTRUCTIONS

If a vehicle starts a Movement Step touching an obstruction, that vehicle **must** ignore the obstruction for that Movement Step.

When a vehicle is ignoring an obstacle, it mostly doesn't collide with it, but they are some exceptions.

Ignoring obstructions in this way may seem a little unrealistic, but the alternative is less fun.

IGNORING OBSTRUCTIONS EXAMPLES

Sometimes the rules will instruct you to ignore obstructions during a movement, most often when you start an activation in contact with another vehicle. In these cases, place the vehicle into its Final Position, even if the ignored obstruction is overlapping the movement template.

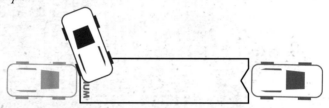

In example A, Blue began its activation in contact with Red, and so is ignoring Red. Blue moves into Final Position as if Red wasn't there.

Occasionally, the movement will still be interrupted by another obstruction that is not being ignored.

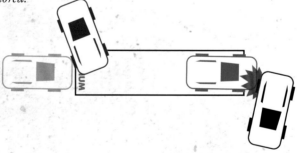

In example B, Blue began its activation in contact with Red, and so is ignoring Red. Black is obstructing Blue's Final Position. Blue attempts to move into its Final Position but collides with Black.

In example C, Blue begins its activation in contact with Red, and so is ignoring Red. Black is interrupting Blue's movement, but when attempted: Blue cannot fit between Red and Black. Following the rules for Multiple Obstructions (see page 46), Blue is moved backwards along the movement template until it is not overlapping any obstruction (even one that it is ignoring), which results in Blue ending up back in its starting position! Blue doesn't actually move. However, no Collision is triggered, as Blue is ignoring Red.

DESTRUCTIBLE OBSTACLES

Some obstacles are Destructible, (see also Terrain, page 86). Destructible obstacles are removed after resolving a Collision with them, leaving the way clear for the active vehicle to continue moving after the Collision.

If the active vehicle's movement is interrupted by a Destructible obstacle, check if the movement is still interrupted after resolving the Collision. If the movement is still interrupted after resolving the Collision and removing the obstacle, find the new Interrupted Final Position. If the movement is no longer interrupted after resolving the Collision, place the vehicle in its Final Position. In this way, a movement can be interrupted multiple times and trigger multiple Collisions.

Wrecks are destructible obstructions, so you can drive through them on your Movement Step, obviously taking the Hazards and possible damage from the Collision.

DESTRUCTIBLE OBSTACLE EXAMPLE

In this example, Black selects a Turn movement template, and places it so that it overlaps a destructible Lightweight obstacle. The obstacle causes the movement to be interrupted, and so Black is moved along the template until it touches the obstacle. This, temporarily, position becomes the Interrupted Final Position. A Collision is now resolved with the obstacle, and then the obstacle is removed because of the Destructible rule.

After the Collision is resolved, the player checks the movement again and, with the obstacle now removed, Black finds the way clear to her Final Position, which she now moves into.

SLIDING INTO OBSTRUCTIONS

If a vehicle's movement is interrupted on its Slide template, Slide the vehicle sideways into the obstruction in order to find its Interrupted Final Position. If a vehicle's movement is interrupted before reaching the Slide Exit Position, find the Interrupted Final Position as normal.

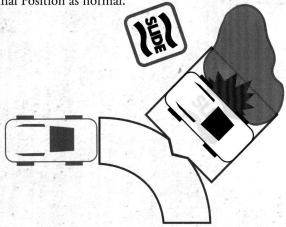

The part of the movement template beyond the Slide Exit Point is ignored for all game purposes. Only the part of the movement template up to the Slide Exit Point, and the Slide template, now count as the vehicle's movement template for the purposes of determining if the movement is interrupted.

If the Slide is coming off a straight template, attempt to pivot the vehicle by 90 degrees as soon as the centre of the vehicle is centred over the Slide Exit Position. If rotating the vehicle in this way causes any part of the active vehicle to touch an obstruction that it is not ignoring, then the movement is interrupted, and this becomes the vehicle's Interrupted Final Position.

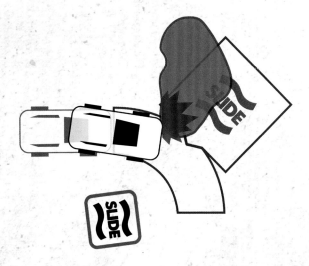

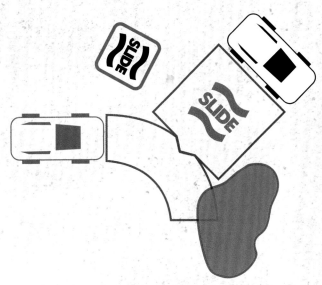

Congratulations! You now have a PhD in "Final Position". Have fun!

COLLISIONS

When two vehicles crash into each other, or a vehicle collides with a bit of scenery, a Collision occurs. Collisions interrupt the normal course of play and must be resolved as soon as the next Collision Window occurs. Resolve the Collision before continuing the active vehicle's activation or forced move.

COLLISION WINDOWS

Collisions only occur during Collision Windows. To make it clear when Collisions can occur, look out for the **COLLISION WINDOWS** noted in the various timing steps throughout the rules.

If you think two vehicles have collided, be sure to step through the timing steps in the back of this book and only trigger the Collision when a Collision Window is indicated.

RESOLVING A COLLISION

To resolve a Collision, follow these steps:

1. Determine orientation.
2. Active vehicle declares reaction.
3. Passive vehicle or obstacle declares reaction.
4. Roll any Smash Attacks.
5. Roll any evades.
6. Apply un-cancelled hits.
7. Gain Hazard Tokens.

ORIENTATION

Every Collision has an orientation. Check the relative facings of the vehicles involved in the Collision to determine its orientation.

HEAD-ON

If the point of contact on **both** vehicles is along their front edge, then the orientation of the Collision is Head-On.

T-BONE

If the point of contact on **either** vehicle is along its side edge, then the orientation of the Collision is T-Bone.

TAILGATE

If the point of contact on **either** vehicle is along the rear edge, then the orientation of the Collision is Tailgate.

If the orientation of the Collision is a Tailgate and the vehicle for which the point of contact is on the rear edge (the "front" vehicle) is in a higher current Gear than the other vehicle, both vehicles must declare Evade as their reaction, as the front vehicle is moving away too fast for the other vehicle to be able to ram it.

STRIKING A CORNER

If the orientation of a Collision is ever unclear, apply the following rules:

- If the point of contact for a vehicle is on the corner of its front and side edges, then the point of contact counts as being on its front edge.
- If the point of contact for a vehicle is on the corner of its rear and side edges, then the point of contact counts as being on its side edge.
- If the active vehicle is moving in reverse, then treat the rear-edge of that vehicle as its front-edge.

REVERSING VEHICLES

If a vehicle either is currently or most recently moved in Reverse, treat the rear-edge of that vehicle as its front-edge for the purposes of determining Collision orientation. This is a sort of "you'll know it when you see it" situation, and the Rule of Carnage applies.

REACTIONS

When a Collision occurs, the players controlling the participants in the Collision take it in turns to declare a reaction for each participant, starting with the vehicle whose movement caused the Collision to occur and proceeding clockwise. The player must declare one of either Smash Attack or Evade as their reaction.

ROLL SMASH ATTACKS AND EVADES

After declaring reactions, any player that declared a Smash Attack must roll to attack. See Smash Attacks, page 54.

If a player declares that they will make a Smash Attack, they will lose the option to evade any incoming Smash Attacks. Similarly, if a player declares an Evade reaction, they will be able to attempt to evade the damage from any incoming Smash Attack, but will lose the option to attack back.

GAIN HAZARD TOKENS

As the last step in the resolution of a Collision, all vehicles involved in the Collision gain 2 Hazard Tokens.

If **both** participants in the ollision choose evade as their reaction, then all vehicles involved in the Collision gain 1 Hazard Token each instead.

COLLISIONS WITH OBSTACLES

If a vehicle collides with an obstacle, the obstacle **always** declares a Smash Attack

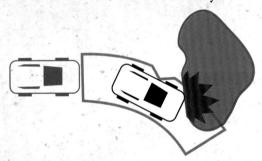

as its reaction. If a vehicle collides with an obstacle, the Collision always counts as a Head-On Collision, wherein the obstacle counts as Gear 0, with a weight according to its type. (See Obstacles, Page 87). If a vehicle collides with a destructible obstacle, remove the obstacle from play immediately after resolving the Collision.

After a Collision, the participants are likely left in contact with each other, unless one or both is Wrecked or later suffers a Wipeout. Remember that a vehicle in contact with an obstacle is Distracted and doesn't get to attack in the Attack Step. Also remember that if a vehicle starts a Movement Step touching an obstruction, such as another vehicle, that vehicle must ignore the obstruction for that Movement Step.

SMASH ATTACKS

A Smash Attack is a type of attack made as part of resolving a Collision.

CALCULATING ATTACK DICE

The number of attack dice rolled during a Smash Attack depends on the orientation of the Collision, and the relative weights of the participants.

If both parties choose to make a Smash Attack, each participant calculates their attack dice separately, but the orientation will be the same for both parties.

If the calculation of the number of attack dice for the Smash Attack results in zero or fewer attack dice, that vehicle rolls no attack dice, but still counts as having made a Smash Attack.

SMASH ATTACK DICE TABLE	
Orientation	**Smash Attack Dice**
Head On	Sum of Current Gears: Each vehicle uses their current Gear plus the other participant's current Gear.
T-bone	Vehicle's Own Current Gear
Tailgate	Difference in Current Gears: Each vehicle uses the faster participant's current Gear minus the slower participant's current Gear, to a minimum of zero.

WEIGHT DIFFERENCE

When calculating the attack dice in a Smash Attack, compare the weights of the two vehicles.

SMASH ATTACK WEIGHT DIFFERENCE TABLE	
Bonus	Bonus Smash Attack Dice
1 Class Heavier	+2 attack dice
2 Classes Heavier	+4 attack dice
1 Class Lighter	-1 attack die
2 Classes Lighter	-2 attack dice

If one vehicle is a single weight-class heavier (i.e. Middleweight compared to Lightweight, or Heavyweight compared to Middleweight) then the heavier vehicle gains +2 attack dice and the lighter vehicle suffers -1 attack die.

If one vehicle is two weight-classes heavier (i.e. Heavyweight compared to Lightweight) then the heavier vehicle gains +4 attack dice and the lighter vehicle suffers -2 attack dice.

Obstacles have a weight, as vehicles do. Solid immovable features, such as walls, buildings, and rocks are Heavyweight. Less substantial features, such as oil barrels, crash barriers, and lampposts are Middleweight. Lightweight obstacles are presumably fruit stalls, or workmen carrying sheets of glass.

RESOLVE SMASH ATTACKS

ROLL ATTACK DICE

Roll the attack dice. Any rolls of 4+ result in a hit on the target. Each natural "6" rolled on an attack dice causes a Critical Hit and causes the target to suffer two hits instead of one.

ROLL EVADE DICE

After calculating the number of hits, the target may make a single Evade attempt if the vehicle declared an Evade reaction.

To Evade: the target's controller rolls a number of Evade dice equal to the vehicle's current Gear. Any die that rolls a 6+ cancels one hit that the vehicle would have received from the attacks. After discounting hits cancelled by evading, remove 1 Hull Point from the target for each un-cancelled hit on the target.

APPLY UN-CANCELLED HITS

When resolving the Smash Attacks in a Collision, hits are applied after **all** the attack dice and Evade dice have been rolled. Damage from Smash Attacks in a Collision is simultaneously applied to both participants.

EXAMPLE COLLISION

A Middleweight car in Gear 5 activates and drives right into the side of a Lightweight buggy in Gear 2. The front of the car is touching the side of the buggy, and so the Collision is a T-Bone.

The player controlling the car chooses to make a Smash Attack, and the player controlling the buggy decides to play it safer and Evade. The player controlling the car could have chosen to Evade, maybe if she already had 4 Hazard Tokens and hoped to avoid a Wipeout. The player controlling the buggy could have declared a Smash Attack instead, but would only have rolled 1 attack die (Gear 2 minus 1 for the weight difference).

With the car choosing to make a Smash Attack and the buggy choosing to Evade, the player controlling the car now calculates her Smash Attack dice, 5 dice for her current Gear (as this is a T-Bone), plus 2 dice for being one weight class heavier. She now rolls her 7-attack dice, needing 4 on each, with 6s doing double. She rolls 1, 1, 2, 4, 4, 5, and 6, meaning three normal hits and one critical hit, for a total of 5 hits.

The player controlling the buggy now rolls his Evade, rolling 2 dice because the buggy is in Gear 2, and hoping for 6s. He lucks out and rolls a 3 and a 6, so one of the 5 hits is cancelled. The player crosses off 4 Hull Points from the dashboard of the buggy for the 4 un-cancelled hits.

Finally, both vehicles get 2 Hazard Tokens each, which may cause trouble next activation. The car cannot shoot in the Attack Step of this activation, as it is Distracted.

EXAMPLE OF PLAY

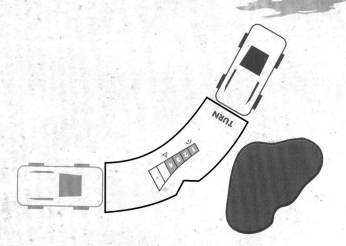

It is Gear Phase 1. Both cars are in Gear 1. The Blue player has Pole Position and so gets the first opportunity to activate a vehicle. She chooses her Blue car and selects the Turn template, placing it in front of the car.

This movement template is Trivial in Gear 1, as indicated by the little Shift icon on the template. Instead of rolling any Skid Dice, Blue chooses to use the free Shift from the template to change up in to Gear 2, gaining one Hazard Token.

In her Attack Step, Blue checks that the Red car is within Medium range and declares that she will use both crew to fire Handguns at it. She rolls 2D6, which come up a "3" and a "6". The "3" is a miss, but the "6" is a Critical Hit, and scores two hits on Red. The Red car is still in Gear 1 and so rolls a single Evade dice. Red is lucky and rolls a "6", which cancels one of the two hits. The remaining hit does one damage to the Red car.

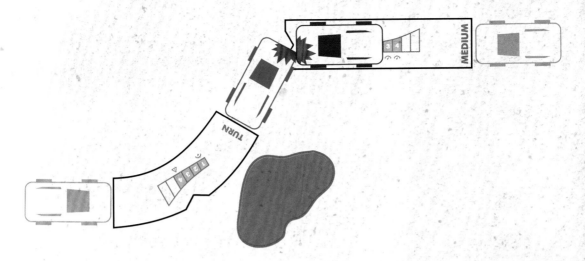

It is now Red's turn to activate a vehicle. She points at the Red car and picks up the medium straight. Placing it down, it is immediately clear that there's going to be a Collision, just as she planned. This movement template is Trivial in Gear 1, but Red wants to increase her speed, to ensure maximum carnage in the ensuing head-on crash. She declares and rolls three Skid Dice, which is the maximum her Handling of 3 will allow. She rolls two Shifts and a Slide. She uses the free Shift from the template to cancel the Slide result and uses the two Shifts from the Skid Dice to move up Gear twice, gaining two Hazard Tokens. Red is now in Gear 3.

As Red's movement template or Final Position overlaps an obstruction (Blue's car), she pushes the vehicle as far down the template as it will go and resolves a Collision. Red declares a Smash Attack, as does Blue. The vehicles are both Middleweight, and as Red has crashed her front edge into a corner on Blue's front edge, the Collision is Head-on.

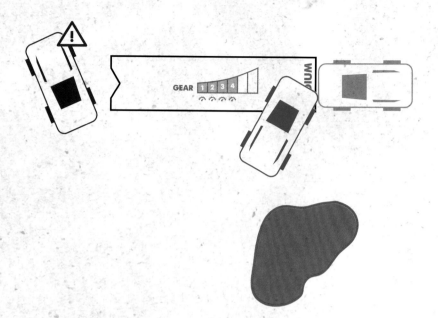

Because of this, the vehicles add their Gears together, and both cars roll (Gear 2 + Gear 3) five attack dice for their Smash Attacks. Neither car gets to roll Evades, as neither declared an Evade reaction. Red rolls five hits on Blue, and Blue rolls three hits back on Red. Both check off the lost Hull Points on their dashboards. Finally, both cars receive two Hazard Tokens for being in a road traffic accident. Red is now on 4 Hazard Tokens.

With no-one left to activate in Gear Phase 1, play proceeds to Gear Phase 2. Both Red and Blue are currently in Gear 2 (or higher), so both will get the chance to activate this Gear Phase. Pole Position has moved to Red, so she moves the first vehicle.

As the Red car is beginning its activation in contact with the Blue car, it ignores Blue during this Movement Step. Red selects the Medium Straight template again and puts it down, ignoring Blue. The ever impetuous Red again rolls all three of her Skid Dice, hoping for a Slide and a Spin that could give her the movement to bring her front-mounted machine guns to bare on Blue. She rolls her dice and gets two Hazard results and a Spin. This isn't what she was looking for, so she decides to Push It. Whereby placing another Hazard Token on her dashboard to pick up and reroll the two dice showing Hazard Results. Disaster! They both come up Spins on the second roll! Red now has three Spin results and only one Shift result to cancel them out. She cannot Push It again and is already sitting on 5 Hazards Tokens. She can't avoid a Wipeout at this point.

In order to reduce the chance of Flipping during the Wipeout, Red decides to use her one Shift result to change down into Gear 2, taking her sixth hazard. She then gains the three hazards from her three Spins and moves into her Final Position at the end of the template. She resolves a desultory Spin once in her Final Position but it's not going to matter, she's on 8 hazards and suffers a Wipeout.

First, she rolls her Flip check and gets a 5, so no Flip occurs. Next, she resets her current Gear to 1 and discards all her Hazard Tokens. Finally, Blue spins Red's car on the spot to face in an unhelpful direction. Red isn't going to get another chance to activate this round, so it's over to Blue to see if she can use the temporary advantage to bring the heat on Red....

SETTING UP A GAME

In order to play a game of *Gaslands*, first build some teams to an agreed maximum number of Cans, and then select (or roll for) the scenario. The scenario will tell you how to set up the table, deploy your vehicles, and assign Pole Position.

BUILDING A TEAM

Gaslands has a simple and flexible system for creating and customising teams. For your first couple of games, we recommend you give each player a single car and a single buggy, both armed with a single front-facing machine gun. That will get you up and running as you learn the basic mechanics of the game. Once you are comfortable with the rules of the game, and want to create your own teams, turn to page 63 for the full rules for building custom teams.

CHOOSING A SCENARIO

Either play the Street Race scenario or turn to page 122 to select one of the many other *Gaslands* scenarios.

STREET RACE

The Street Race scenario is a simplified version of the Death Race scenario that appears on page 124. This scenario is intended as an introduction to the *Gaslands* game, allowing new players to get to grips with the basic rules without adding anything extra. Once you are comfortable with the rules of *Gaslands*, we recommend you play the proper Death Race scenario in place of this one, as that provides a number of extra rules that make *Gaslands* racing more exciting.

TEAMS

Give each player a team of one Car and one Buggy, both armed with a front-mounted machine gun.

SETUP

Set up a pair of objects (flags or crates) a long straight apart to create a Starting Line and another pair to create a Finish Line. Make sure the start and finish line are at least three long straights away from each other. Lay out some terrain, such as rock, crates, or barriers to break up the route from the start line to the finish.

POLE POSITION

Roll off to determine who has Pole Position. The player with Pole Position deploys the first vehicle and activates the first vehicle. At the end of each Gear Phase, pass Pole Position clockwise.

STARTING LINE

Starting with the player in Pole Position, players take it in turns to place a vehicle anywhere touching the starting grid, not touching any other vehicle.

VICTORY

The first vehicle to cross the Finish Line wins the race and the game is over. If there is only one player with active vehicles in play at any point, the game ends and that player wins.

CREATING A TEAM

The previous sections, "Basic Rules" and "Additional Rules", covered everything you need to know to play a game of *Gaslands*. If you haven't played your first game yet, you already know everything you need to go do that.

All of the rules beyond this point are optional, and will make more sense after you have a couple of games under your belt to cement the core rules. These optional rules will be waiting for you, ready to make your *Gaslands* games more awesome by providing more customisation, more depth and more madcap ways to enjoy the game.

CUSTOMISING YOUR TEAM

After your first couple of games, you will very likely want to start building your own personalised *Gaslands* teams. As you customise and maybe paint up your toy cars, *Gaslands* gives you quick and easy way to represent your own unique vehicles on the tabletop.

TEAM SIZE

Before each game, agree a team size with your fellow players. This is the total number of Cans you have available to build and equip all your vehicles. A good team size is between 25 and 100 Cans for each player.

50 Cans each is generally agreed to be the "standard" game size, which roughly buys you two to four vehicles and a bit of kit, but this should not be considered a rule!

CHOOSE A SPONSOR

If you are using sponsors (see page 91), select a sponsor for your team before you start, which grants you a set of sponsored perks and determines which perk classes are available to you.

BUILD VEHICLES

Each player buys and customises vehicles up to the agreed team size. Building a vehicle is as simple as selected a vehicle type, arming it with weapons and upgrades up to its build slot limit, and personalising it further with perks from the sponsor's permitted perk classes.

BUILDING A VEHICLE

To build a new vehicle, follow these steps:

- Choose a vehicle type.
- Add weapons, noting the build slots required, and declaring a facing for each weapon.
- Add upgrades, noting the build slots required.
- Add perks from the permitted perk classes.

COST

Cans of gasoline are the new gold standard and are traded for parts and services throughout the wasted Earth. Every vehicle, weapon, upgrade, and perk have an associated cost. This cost is the number of Cans required to purchase the item when building your team.

BUILD SLOTS

Each vehicle has a number of Build Slots. When building a vehicle, weapons and upgrades require a number of available build slots to be fitted. Once weapons and upgrades have used up a vehicle's available build slots no more may be fitted.

FACING

When arming a vehicle with a weapon, the player must declare a single facing for that weapon. A weapon's facing determines the weapon's Arc of Fire.

When you purchase a weapon or upgrade and declare the side-mounted facing, you do not have to declare a specific side: the weapon or upgrade counts as being mounted on both sides.

PERKS

Vehicles may only purchase perks from those perks classes lists under their chosen sponsor. There is no limit to the number of perks each vehicle can have. Each perk may only be purchased once for each vehicle.

BASIC VEHICLE TYPES

These basic vehicle types describe the majority of the cars in your toy box. These vehicle types are intended to be quite broad brushes, and you can use each type to represent quite a wide array of makes and models. If you have a vehicle in front of you that doesn't fit any of these basic types, check out the Advanced Vehicle Types section on page 68 for more options.

BASIC VEHICLE TYPE TABLE								
Vehicle Type	Weight	Hull	Handling	Max Gear	Crew	Build Slots	Special Rules	Cost
Buggy	Lightweight	6	4	6	2	2	Roll Cage.	6
Car	Middleweight	10	3	5	2	2		12
Performance Car	Middleweight	8	4	6	1	2	Slip Away.	15
Truck	Middleweight	12	2	4	3	3		15
Heavy Truck	Heavyweight	14	2	3	4	5		25
Bus	Heavyweight	16	2	3	8	3		30

BUGGY

Roll Cage: When this vehicle suffers a flip, this vehicle may choose to ignore the 2 hits received from the flip.

PERFORMANCE CAR

Slip Away: If this vehicle is targeted with a tailgate or T-Bone Smash Attack, and this vehicle declares Evade as its reaction, this vehicle may perform a free activation immediately after the active vehicle completes its activation.

This free activation does not count as the vehicle's activation this Gear Phase.

Use of the Slip Away rule can allow this vehicle to activate twice in a row, twice in one Gear Phase, or once in a Gear Phase that it does not qualify to activate in (and it might then change Gear and qualify late in that phase). Friendly vehicles can trigger this effect.

BASIC WEAPONS

Gaslands wouldn't be good television without guns! Here are the basic weapon types for you to use in your first few games. Once you are comfortable with the shooting rules, go ahead and dig into the Advanced Weapons rules on page 72 for more deadly and explosive weaponry.

When building a vehicle, weapons have two other statistics you need to know about:

BUILD SLOTS

The cost value determines the number of free build slots required to arm a vehicle with this weapon.

COST

The cost value determines the cost in Cans of arming a vehicle with this weapon.

BASIC WEAPON TABLE					
Weapon Name	Range	Attack Dice	Special Rules	Build Slots	Cost
Handgun	Medium	1D6	Crew Fired.	-	-
Machine Gun	Double	2D6		1	2
Heavy Machine Gun	Double	3D6		1	3
Minigun	Double	4D6		1	5

Crew Fired: A weapon that is Crew Fired benefits from a 360-degree Arc of Fire, and does not need to declare a facing when purchased.

ADVANCED RULES

All the rules in this section are optional, but will provide a host of new and awesome options to make your teams and your games more cinematic and explosive.

ADVANCED VEHICLE TYPES

The basic vehicle types are designed to cover the majority of conversions possible with toy cars. However, enthusiastic rummagers in supermarket toy bins and thrift store crates may unearth delights that aren't covered by the existing basic vehicle types. The section provides an expanded set of vehicle types to allow you to include a broader range of vehicles in your games.

ADVANCED VEHICLE TYPES TABLE								
Vehicle Type	Weight	Hull	Handling	Max Gear	Crew	Build Slots	Special Rules	Cost
Drag Racer	Lightweight	4	4	6	1	2	Jet Engine.	5
Bike	Lightweight	4	5	6	1	1	Full Throttle. Pivot.	5
Bike with Sidecar	Lightweight	4	5	6	2	2	Full Throttle. Pivot.	8
Ice Cream Truck	Middleweight	10	2	4	2	2	Infuriating Jingle.	8
Gyrocopter	Middleweight	4	4	6	1	0	Airwolf. Airborne.	10
Ambulance	Middleweight	12	2	5	3	3	Uppers. Downers.	20
Monster Truck	Heavyweight	10	3	4	2	2	All Terrain. Up and Over.	25
Helicopter	Heavyweight	8	3	4	3	4	Airwolf. Airborne. Restricted	30
Tank	Heavyweight	20	4	3	3	4	Pivot. Up and Over. All Terrain. Turret. Restricted	40
War Rig	Heavyweight	26	2	4	5	5	See War Rig rules.	40

You will find a blank dashboard card in the back of this book. Fill it in with the stats of the vehicle you have chosen. You can also find a full set of vehicle dashboards to download on the Gaslands website.

RESTRICTED VEHICLE TYPES

Some vehicle types are Restricted. If you are playing with Sponsor rules (see page 91), Helicopters and Tanks cannot be purchased as standard. Only teams with an appropriate Sponsor perk may purchase those vehicle types, (see Sponsors, page 91).

Whilst Helicopters and Tanks are restricted in games that use Sponsors, you can of course ignore this restriction if you like, and play with the full set of vehicle types. Your table, your rules.

AMBULANCE
UPPERS

If this vehicle is involved in a Collision in which both vehicles declare an Evade, both vehicles must declare a single change Gear up immediately after the Collision is resolved (gaining a Hazard Token as normal). If either vehicle is already at its max Gear, the change of Gear does not affect that vehicle's current Gear, but that vehicle does gain a Hazard Token.

DOWNERS

When this vehicle is involved in a Collision during its activation in which it declares a Smash Attack, the target vehicle does not gain any Hazard Tokens from the Collision and instead discards 2 Hazard Tokens. Then reduce the target vehicle's Crew Value by 1 until the end of the Gear Phase.

BIKE AND BIKE WITH SIDECAR
FULL THROTTLE

This vehicle considers the Long Straight movement template to be permitted in any Gear. The Long Straight is not considered either Hazardous or Trivial in any Gear.

PIVOT

At the start of this vehicle's activation, if this vehicle's current Gear is 1, this vehicle may make a pivot about its centre to face any direction. This pivot cannot cause a Collision and cannot leave this vehicle touching an obstruction.

DRAG RACER
JET ENGINE

A vehicle with a jet engine counts as having a Nitro Booster with infinite ammo tokens. This means this vehicle automatically Explodes when it is Wrecked. A vehicle with a jet engine must use Nitro Booster every time it activates.

HELICOPTER AND GYROCOPTER
AIRBORNE

This vehicle ignores non-tall obstructions, dropped weapons, and terrain at all times, except when checking for Cover, and when targeting other vehicles in its Attack Step.

   Other vehicles ignore this vehicle at all times, except that other vehicles may target this vehicle during their Attack Steps. This vehicle cannot be involved in Collisions.

AIRWOLF

At the start of this vehicle's activation, this vehicle may gain 2 Hazard Tokens to make a single pivot about its centre point, up to 90 degrees.

BOMBS AWAY

When purchasing weapons for this vehicle, this vehicle may count dropped weapons as requiring 0 build slots. This vehicle may attack with any number of dropped weapons in a single Attack Step.

ICE CREAM TRUCK
INFURIATING JINGLE

Vehicles that target this vehicle with a Smash Attack during a Collision gain no Hazard Tokens during step 6 of the Collision resolution.

© James Hall

MONSTER TRUCK

ALL TERRAIN

This vehicle may ignore the penalties for rough and treacherous surfaces.

UP AND OVER

During this vehicle's Movement Step, after resolving a Collision with an obstruction of a lower weight class, this vehicle may declare that it is going "Up and Over". If it does, it may ignore the obstruction for the remainder of its Movement Step, as it drives right over the top of it. This vehicle cannot use this ability to ignore another vehicle with the Up and Over special rule.

TANK

ALL TERRAIN

This vehicle may ignore the penalties for rough and treacherous surfaces.

PIVOT

At the start of this vehicle's activation, if this vehicle's current Gear is 1, this vehicle may make a pivot about its centre to face any direction. This pivot cannot cause a Collision and cannot leave this vehicle touching an obstruction.

TURRET

This vehicle may count one weapon as turret-mounted without paying for the upgrade.

UP AND OVER

During this vehicle's Movement Step, after resolving a Collision with an obstruction of a lower weight class, this vehicle may declare that it is going "Up and Over". If it does, it may ignore the obstruction for the remainder of its Movement Step, as it drives right over the top of it. This vehicle cannot use this ability to ignore another vehicle with the "Up and Over" special rule.

WAR RIG

The War Rig has multiple special rules. See the War Rig section on page 116 for details.

ADVANCED WEAPONS

In this section, you will find a bountiful armoury of implements of carnage, from the explosive to the exotic.

ADVANCED WEAPON TABLE					
Weapon Name	Range	Attack Dice	Special Rules	Build Slots	Cost
125mm Cannon	Double	8D6	Ammo 3. Blast. See special rules.	3	6
Arc Lightning Projector	Double	6D6	Ammo 1. Electrical. See special rules.	2	6**
Bazooka	Double	3D6	Ammo 3. Blast.	2	4
BFG	Double	10D6	Ammo 1. See special rules.	3	1
Combat Laser	Double	3D6	Splash. See special rules.	1	5
Death Ray	Double	3D6	Ammo 1. Electrical. See special rules.	1	3
Flamethrower	Large Burst	6D6	Ammo 3. Splash. Fire. Indirect.	2	4
Grabber Arm	Short	3D6	See special rules.	1	6
Grav Gun	Double	(3D6)	Ammo 1. Electrical. See special rules.	1	2**
Harpoon	Double	(5D6)	See special rules.	1	2
Kinetic Super Booster	Double	(6D6)	Ammo 1. Electrical. See special rules.	2	6**
Magnetic Jammer	Double	-	Electrical. See special rules.	-	2**
Mortar	Double	4D6	Ammo 3. Indirect.	1	4
Rockets	Double	6D6	Ammo 3.	2	5
Thumper	Medium	-	Ammo 1. Electrical. Indirect. 360-degree. See special rules.	2	4**
Wall of Amplifiers	Medium	-	360-degree arc of fire. See special rules.	3	4
Wreck Lobber	Double/ Dropped	-	Ammo 3. See special rules.	4	4
Wrecking Ball	Short	*	*See special rules.	3	2
** Mishkin-sponsored teams only.					

125MM CANNON

A tank gun is a ridiculous weapon for a civilian vehicle to carry. When fired, the active vehicle immediately gains 2 Hazard Tokens if it is not a Tank.

ARC LIGHTNING PROJECTOR

Mishkin-sponsored teams only. The Arc Lightning Projector is a dangerous weapon that can arc electricity across multiple conductive targets. After damaging a target, this vehicle **must** immediately attack another target within Short range and 360-degree Arc of Fire of the current target (including this vehicle). This chain-reaction continues until the weapon fails to damage a target, or there are no further viable targets. This vehicle can target friendly vehicles with the Arc Lightning Projector. This vehicle cannot target the same vehicle twice in a single Attack Step with the Arc Lightning Projector.

BFG

When this weapon is fired, the vehicle makes an immediately forced move medium straight backwards, reduced to Gear 1 and gains 3 Hazard Tokens. Front mounted only.

DEATH RAY

Mishkin-sponsored teams only. If this weapon scores five or more un-cancelled hits on the target during a single attack, instead of causing damage, the target car is immediately removed from play (although it counts as having been Wrecked for the purposes of Audience Votes, scenario rules, etc.).

GRABBER ARM

If this vehicle attacks a target vehicle of the same weight class or lighter with the Grabber Arm and scores one or more un-cancelled hits, the controller of the active vehicle may place the target vehicle anywhere within Short range of the target vehicle's original position. The target vehicle may be pivoted to face any direction. This movement causes a Collision Window.

GRAV GUN

Mishkin-sponsored teams only. If this weapon scores one or more un-cancelled hits on the target, instead of causing damage the attacking vehicle's controller must choose one of the following: until the end of the target's next activation the target counts as one weight class heavier or until the end of the target's next activation the target counts as one weight class lighter.

© Jake Zettelmaier

HARPOON

This weapon's hits do not cause damage. Instead, the first un-cancelled hit on the target spins the target vehicle on the spot to either face directly away from or directly towards the attacking vehicle, whichever requires the smallest degree of rotation, as the harpoon catches and the chain goes taut. This triggers a Collision Window.

The second and subsequent un-cancelled hits on the target then each cause the target to make a forced Short Straight move towards the attacker, as the harpoon reels the target in.

If the target is a heavier weight class than the attacker, it is the attacking vehicle that is spun and moved towards the target vehicle instead.

KINETIC SUPER BOOSTER

Mishkin-sponsored teams only. The Kinetic Super Booster is a bizarre electrical weapon that transfers a jolt of kinetic energy to the target. The target of a Super Booster attack suffers no damage, but instead immediately increases its current Gear by one for every successful hit, without gaining Hazard Tokens. The Super Booster may not increase a vehicle's current Gear beyond its max Gear.

MAGNETIC JAMMER

Mishkin-sponsored teams only. The target vehicle may not discard ammo tokens during its next activation.

THUMPER

Mishkin-sponsored teams only. This weapon does not need to declare a facing when purchased.

The Thumper is a powerful sonic device that emits a shock wave that hurls nearby vehicles into the air. When this vehicle declares an attack with the Thumper, every other vehicle (friend or foe) within Medium range of this vehicle in a 360-degree Arc of Fire immediately makes a Flip check, in which they count their current Gear as 2 higher, up to a maximum of 6.

WALL OF AMPLIFIERS

This weapon does not require a target. When fired, this weapon automatically causes one hit to **every** vehicle within Medium range and within a 360-degree Arc of Fire. These hits do not cause damage and may be Evaded. For each un-cancelled hit on a vehicle, choose one: either discard 1 Hazard Token from the vehicle or add 1 Hazard Token to the vehicle.

WRECK LOBBER

It was inevitable that someone would invent a gun that shoots cars instead of bullets.

Trebuchet: The Wreck Lobber does not require a target. When it is fired, place a marker the size of a penny within Double range of the Wreck Lobber's fire arc. Roll a Skid Die.

- On a Shift result: place the wreck of a Car touching the marker and trigger a Collision Window.
- On a Spin or Slide result: the player to the left of the active player must place the wreck anywhere within Short range of the marker and trigger a Collision Window.
- On a Hazard Result: the player to the left of the active player must place the wreck touching the active vehicle and trigger a Collision Window.

Low-loader: If this vehicle collides with a wreck, it may gain 1 Ammo Token for the Wreck Lobber.

Dumper: This vehicle may fire the Wreck Lobber as a rear-mounted dropped weapon instead of using the Trebuchet rules above. In this case, the wreck of a car is placed touching the rear of the active vehicle, and no Collision Window is triggered.

WRECKING BALL

This weapon does not require a target. When fired, this vehicle must immediately engage in a T-Bone Collision with every vehicle and Destructible obstacle within Short range of it, in a 360-degree Arc of Fire, in an order chosen by this vehicle's controller.

During these Collisions, all vehicles involved count as having no weapons or perks except this one and all other vehicles must declare an Evade reaction. During each these Collisions this vehicle gains 2 Smash Attack dice. This vehicle does not gain Hazard Tokens during these Collisions. Collisions triggered by the Wrecking Ball do not benefit from effects from upgrades, such as Rams or Exploding Rams.

CREW FIRED WEAPONS

The wild-eyed crews of *Gaslands* vehicles sport a deadly array of hand-held day-ruiners.

CREW FIRED WEAPONS TABLE					
Weapon Name	Range	Attack Dice	Special Rules	Build Slots	Cost
Blunderbuss	Small Burst	2D6	Crew Fired. Splash.	-	2
Gas Grenades	Medium	(1D6)	Ammo 5. Crew Fired. Indirect. Blitz. See special rules.	-	1
Grenades	Medium	1D6	Ammo 5. Crew Fired. Blast. Indirect. Blitz.	-	1
Magnum	Double	1D6	Crew Fired. Blast.	-	3
Molotov Cocktails	Medium	1D6	Ammo 5. Crew Fired. Fire. Indirect. Blitz.	-	1
Shotgun	Long	*	Crew Fired. See special rules.	-	4
Steel Nets	Short	(3D6)	Crew Fired. Blast. See special rules.	-	2
Submachine Gun	Medium	3D6	Crew fired.	-	5

CREW FIRED

A weapon that is Crew Fired benefits from a 360-degree Arc of Fire and does not need to declare a facing when purchased.

GAS GRENADES

If this weapon scores one or more un-cancelled hits on the target, instead of causing damage, reduce the target's Crew Value by 1 for each un-cancelled hit, to a minimum of 0, until the end of the Gear Phase.

STEEL NETS

This weapon's hits do not cause damage. Hits will add Hazard Tokens as a result of the Blast special rule as normal.

SHOTGUN

When attacking with this weapon, roll 3D6 attack dice if the target is within Short range, 2D6 attack dice if the target is within Medium range, and 1D6 attack dice if the target is within Long range.

DROPPED WEAPONS

You are at the front of the pack. The road is empty ahead of you. Worry not, here's a toolkit of unpleasant things you can do to anyone that gets up too close behind.

DROPPED WEAPONS TABLE					
Weapon Name	Range	Attack Dice	Special Rules	Build Slots	Cost
Caltrop Dropper	Dropped	2D6	Ammo 3. Small Burst. See special rules.	1	1
Glue Dropper	Dropped	-	Ammo 1. See special rules.	1	1
Mine Dropper	Dropped	4D6	Ammo 3. Small Burst. Blast. See special rules.	1	1
Napalm Dropper	Dropped	4D6	Ammo 3. Small Burst. Fire. See special rules.	1	1
Oil Slick Dropper	Dropped	-	Ammo 3. See special rules.	-	2
RC Car Bombs	Dropped	4D6	Ammo 3. See special rules.	-	3
Sentry Gun	Dropped	2D6	Ammo 3. See special rules.	-	3
Smoke Dropper	Dropped	-	Ammo 3. See special rules.	-	1

DROPPED WEAPON RULES

Dropped weapons may not be front-mounted. A vehicle may only attack with a single dropped weapon in a single Attack Step.

To attack with a dropped weapon: place the appropriate shooting template within the weapon's Arc of Fire, and instead of rolling to attack, leave it on the table until instructed otherwise. This dropped weapon template does not count as overlapping the active vehicle.

Leave the dropped weapon template in place when the vehicle next moves. The dropped weapon template remains in play for the rest of the game, unless their specific rules state otherwise.

If a dropped weapon template overlaps a vehicle, or if a vehicle's movement template or Final Position overlaps a dropped weapon template, resolve the dropped weapon's effects against that vehicle in the next Collision Window. Vehicles attacked by a dropped weapon may Evade any hits from that weapon.

If there are multiple dropped weapon templates stacked on top of each other, just resolve each template in order, from the top of the stack to the bottom.

CALTROP DROPPER

The dropped weapon template for this dropped weapon counts as a treacherous surface, (see Terrain, page 86).

The first vehicle affected by this weapon is attacked with a 2D6 attack, then remove the Caltrops template from play.

GLUE DROPPER

The dropped weapon template for the Glue Dropper counts as a treacherous surface. Any vehicle affected by this weapon must reduce its current Gear by 2 at the end of their Movement Step. A single vehicle may not be affected by this weapon two activations in a row.

MINE DROPPER

The first vehicle affected by this weapon is attacked with a 4D6 attack with Blast, then remove the Mine's template from play.

NAPALM DROPPER

The first vehicle affected by this weapon is attacked with a 4D6 attack with Fire, then remove the Napalm template from play.

OIL SLICK DROPPER

The dropped weapon template for the Oil Slick Dropper counts as a treacherous surface, (see Terrain, page 86).

RC CAR BOMBS

Bombs are taped to remote-controlled cars, which are dropped from a vehicle and then piloted to impact.

When attacking with this dropped weapon, place a RC Car (use a tiny car miniature, no larger than 20mm square) so that it is within Short range of the attacking vehicle, and facing in any direction. This placement triggers a Collision Window.

The RC Car counts as a lightweight vehicle in current Gear 3 with 1 Hull Point, 1 Crew and 0 Handling. This tiny car can make shooting attacks but cannot change Gear. Although controlled by the player that dropped it, the RC Car does not count as part of the player's team, and so cannot be used for the purposes of scenario rules, Audience Votes, or perks.

The RC Car is involved in a Collision, it suffers one damage before the Collision is resolved. When the RC Car would be Wrecked, it instead explodes. When the RC Car explodes, it rolls 4D6 attack dice, as if it were a middleweight vehicle.

If the RC Car wipes out, it suffers one damage before the Wipeout is resolved.

SENTRY GUN

When attacking with this dropped weapon, place a Sentry Gun so that it is within Short range of the attacking vehicle.

The Sentry Gun remains in play as a lightweight destructible obstacle. They may be targeted with shooting attacks and have 2 Hull Points.

This Sentry Gun automatically makes a 2D6 shooting attack against any vehicle that ends their Movement Step within Medium range of the Sentry Gun in a 360-degree Arc of Fire. The target may Evade as normal. This Sentry Gun will never target vehicles from the team of the vehicle that dropped it.

Although controlled by the player that dropped it, the Sentry Gun does not count as part of the player's team, and so cannot be used for the purposes of scenario rules, Audience Votes, or perks.

SMOKE DROPPER

This dropped weapon template counts as an obstruction for the purposes of determining Cover.

Whilst a vehicle is in contact with this dropped weapon template, that vehicle counts as distracted.

If any part of a vehicle's movement template or Final Position touches this dropped weapon template, the vehicle gains 1 Hazard Token at the end of its Movement Step.

WEAPON SPECIAL RULES

ATTACKING WITH SPECIAL WEAPONS

Some weapons have special rules that trigger only if the weapon hits or damages the target. When rolling to attack, a player will need to make it clear which dice represent attacks from which weapons, if special rules would apply to those attacks. You might consider using different coloured dice for those special attacks, or rolling them to one side.

© Jake Zettelmaier

AMMO

Some weapons and upgrades have limited fuel or ammunition. A weapon or upgrade with this special rule begins the game with (x) number of Ammo Tokens on its dashboard for that weapon or upgrade, where (x) is the value listed.

Before making an attack with this weapon or using this upgrade, this vehicle must discard an Ammo Token from this weapon or upgrade. If the vehicle cannot discard an Ammo Token, this weapon or upgrade may not be used.

Ammo Tokens are specific to a given weapon or upgrade. A vehicle may not discard Ammo Tokens from one weapon or upgrade to attack with another weapon or use another upgrade.

f you are playing with Audience Votes, you can use Reload to replenish your Ammo Tokens. See page 89 for more information.

BLAST

For every un-cancelled hit caused by a weapon or effect with the Blast rule, the target immediately gains 1 Hazard Token.

BLITZ

This vehicle counts as being armed with a number of copies of this weapon equal to this weapon's remaining Ammo Tokens, where each copy counts as having a single Ammo Token. This means that during its Attack Step, this vehicle may attack with this weapon any number of times, as long as it doesn't attack more times that is has Ammo Tokens, and doesn't attack more times than its Crew Value.

CREW FIRED

A weapon that is Crew Fired benefits from a 360-degre Arc of Fire and does not need to declare a facing when purchased.

FIRE

If a vehicle suffers at least one damage from a weapon or effect with the Fire special rule, it gains the On-Fire rule in addition to suffering damage. A vehicle cannot gain the On-Fire rule a second time.

On Fire: At the start of this vehicle's activation, it loses 1 Hull Point. This vehicle's Smash Attacks count as having the Fire special rule. If this vehicle ever has zero Hazard Tokens, the fire goes out and this vehicle loses the On-Fire rule.

INDIRECT

When making a shooting attack with a weapon with this special rule, the vehicle may ignore Terrain and Cover during that attack.

SPLASH

When a weapon with the Splash rule is used to attack, the weapon must target, and attack, every vehicle beneath the shooting template, including friendly vehicles. Each target must suffer a separate attack from the weapon.

For example, a truck has a side-mounted Flamethrower and is driving besides two enemy cars. The player declares an attack against one of the two cars. He takes the Large Burst template and places it perpendicular with the side of his truck, and touching the side edge of his truck. He is able to catch both enemy cars under the template and so rolls two separate attacks, one against each enemy, with the full 6D6 attack dice against both.

ZERO CREW

Some game effect can reduce a vehicle's Crew Value. When a vehicle with zero Crew is selected to activate, it first automatically changes down one Gear to a minimum of Gear 1. During its Movement Step, only movement templates that are hazardous in the vehicle's current Gear count as permitted. This means in Gear Phases 1 and 2, the player controlling a vehicle will be forced to select movement templates that are not permitted.

VEHICLE UPGRADES

No mechanic that builds vehicles for Gaslands can resist adding a few personal touches.

Upgrades	Special Rules	Build Slots	Cost
	VEHICLE UPGRADE TABLE		
Armour Plating	+2 Hull Points	1	4
Experimental Nuclear Engine	Electrical. See special rules.	-	5**
Experimental Teleporter	Electrical. See special rules.	-	7**
Exploding Ram	Ammo 1. See special rules.	-	3
Extra Crewmember	+1 Crew, up to a maximum of twice the vehicle's starting Crew Value	-	4
Improvised Sludge Thrower	See special rules.	1	2
Nitro Booster	Ammo 1. See special rules.	-	6
Ram	See special rules.	1	4
Roll Cage	See special rules.	1	4
Tank Tracks	-1 Max Gear. +1 Handling. See special rules.	1	4
Turret Mounting for Weapon	Weapon gains 360 arc of fire.	-	(x3)
** Mishkin-sponsored teams only.			

ARMOUR PLATING

The vehicle has been loaded with additional plates and shielding. This vehicle has its Hull Value permanently increased by 2. A single vehicle may be fitted with multiple Armour Plating upgrades for further +2 hull each time.

EXPERIMENTAL NUCLEAR ENGINE

Mishkin-sponsored teams only. This upgrade may not be purchased for lightweight vehicles. A vehicle may only purchase this upgrade once.

Add 2 to this vehicle's max Gear, (up to a maximum of 6). This vehicle considers the Long Straight movement to be permitted in any Gear. The Long Straight is not considered either Hazardous or Trivial in any Gear.

If this vehicle ever fails a Flip check, it is immediately Wrecked and automatically Explodes. When this vehicle Explodes, it counts as Heavyweight.

EXPERIMENTAL TELEPORTER

Mishkin-sponsored teams only. A vehicle may only purchase this upgrade once.

At the start of this vehicle's activation this vehicle may choose to activate the Experimental Teleporter prior to (and in addition to) its normal Movement Step.

When the Experimental Teleporter is activated, this vehicle gains 3 Hazard Tokens, and then rolls a single Skid Die.

If the Skid Dice result is any result other than a Hazard, place this vehicle anywhere within **Medium** range of its current position, not touching an obstruction or terrain, without altering the vehicle's facing. This does not cause a Collision. This vehicle then begins its normal Movement Step from this new location.

If the Skid Dice result is a Hazard, the player to the left of the controller of the vehicle places this vehicle anywhere within **Long** range of its current position, not touching an obstruction or terrain, without altering its facing. This does not cause a Collision.

EXPLODING RAM

When purchasing this upgrade, a facing must be declared for it, as if it was a weapon. A vehicle may only purchase this upgrade once. Lightweight vehicles may not purchase this weapon.

The first time this vehicle is involved in a Collision on the declared facing in a game, this vehicle must declare a Smash Attack (even if the Collision is a Tailgate). During this Smash Attack this vehicle gains +6 attack dice. If any 1s or 2s are rolled on this vehicle's attack dice during this Smash Attack, this vehicle immediately loses one hull point for each 1 or 2 rolled.

A vehicle may equip both a Ram and an Explosive Ram on the same facing, and their effects are cumulative.

EXTRA CREWMEMBER

Each Extra Crewmember purchased increases the vehicles Crew Value by 1. This will increase the number of attacks a vehicle can make in its Attack Step. See Shooting Attacks, page 30.

A vehicle may not purchase more Extra Crewmembers than its starting Crew Value.

For example, a pickup truck, which has a Crew Value of 3, may purchase up to 3 Extra Crewmembers, for a maximum Crew Value of 6.

IMPROVISED SLUDGE THROWER

This vehicle may place the Burst templates for its dropped weapons anywhere that is at least partially within Medium range and 360-degree Arc of Fire of this vehicle.

NITRO BOOSTER

Once per activation, at the start of a Movement Step, this vehicle may declare that it is using a Nitro Booster. If it does, this vehicle makes an immediate forced, Long Straight move forward, and then gains Hazard Tokens until it has 5 Hazard Tokens. It then resolves its Movement Step as normal, except that the vehicle may

not reverse. At the end of a Movement Step in which this vehicle used Nitro Booster, it gains Hazard Tokens until it has 5 Hazard Tokens.

RAM

The Ram can represent a ram, a bulldozer blade, a cow-catcher, a buzz saw, a wrecking ball on a chain, spiked or scythed wheels, metal spikes, or any other vicious or dangerous close combat weapon attached to the vehicle.

When purchasing this upgrade, a facing must be declared for it, as if it was a weapon. A vehicle may only purchase a single Ram on each facing.

When involved in a Collision on the declared facing, this vehicle may add 2 attack dice to its Smash Attack, and this vehicle does not gain any Hazard Tokens as a result of the Collision.

ROLL CAGE

When this vehicle suffers a Flip, this vehicle may choose to ignore the 2 hits received from the Flip.

TANK TRACKS

The vehicle with Tank Tracks has had its wheels replaced with caterpillar tracks. This increases its handling by 1, but reduces its max Gear by 1. This vehicle may also ignore rough and treacherous surfaces.

A vehicle may only purchase this upgrade once. Tanks, Helicopters, and Gyrocopters may not purchase Tank Tracks.

TURRET MOUNTING FOR WEAPON

When purchasing a shooting weapon for a vehicle, players may pay three times the basic cost of the weapon to make it Turret-mounted. A Turret-mounted weapon has a 360-degree Arc of Fire (see Arc of Fire, page 28).

For example, a front-mounted Minigun will cost you 5 Cans, but a Turret-mounted Minigun will cost you 15 Cans.

TERRAIN

A great looking selection of terrain, scenery, and obstructions will improve your *Gaslands* games. Here are some additional effects that you can choose to use to give your games more variety and challenge.

SURFACES

Surfaces are types of terrain that describe the condition of the ground. Surfaces do not count as obstructions.

ROAD

If every part of a vehicle's movement template and Final Position (after resolving all Skid Dice) overlaps a Road Surface, then the vehicle may discard a Hazard Token at the end of this Movement Step.

ROUGH

If any part of a vehicle's movement template or Final Position (after resolving all Skid Dice) overlaps a Rough Surface, the vehicle gains 1 Hazard Token at the end of its Movement Step.

TREACHEROUS

If any part of a vehicle's movement template or Final Position (after resolving all Skid Dice) overlaps a Treacherous Surface, the vehicle gains 2 Hazard Tokens at the end of its Movement Step.

EDGE OF THE TABLE

If any part of a vehicle's movement template (after resolving all Skid Dice) overlaps the edge of the play area, the vehicle is disqualified and removed from play, (unless the scenario specifies otherwise). A disqualified vehicle does not count as Wrecked.

OBSTACLES

Obstacles always count as obstructions.

Obstacles have a weight, as vehicles do. Heavyweight obstacles are solid immovable features, such as walls, buildings, and rocks. Middleweight obstacles are less substantial features, such as oil barrels, crash barriers, and lampposts. Lightweight obstacles are, presumably, fruit stalls or workmen carrying sheets of glass.

TALL

Obstacles may be Tall. If the shooting template overlaps a Tall obstruction before it touches the target, the target cannot be targeted by this weapon. Agree with your fellow players at the start of the game which obstacles are Tall.

DESTRUCTIBLE OBSTACLES

Obstacles may be Destructible. Agree with your fellow players at the start of the game which obstacles are Destructible.

If a vehicle collides with a Destructible obstacle, remove the obstacle from play immediately after resolving the Collision.

VOLATILE OBSTACLES

Obstacles, such as gas canisters or ammo dumps, may be Volatile. Agree with your fellow players at the start of the game which obstacles are Volatile.

When a vehicle collides with a Volatile obstacle, roll a die before declaring reactions. On the roll of a 4+, the Volatile obstacle explodes! Make an attack with Blast rule against each vehicle within Medium range of the exploding volatile obstacle, calculating attack dice based on the weight of the obstacle, as if it was an exploding wreck, then remove the obstacle. See Explosions, page 44.

RAMPS

Agree which terrain items count as a Ramp with your fellow players before the game. Nominate an "entry edge" for the Ramp, which is the bit of the ramp that you drive up on to.

If a vehicle's movement template or Final Position overlaps any edge other than the entry edge, they stop at the edge of the Ramp and roll a D6. If the die roll is equal to or under the vehicle's current Gear: make a Jump, else make a Tumble.

JUMP

The vehicle stops at the edge of the Ramp and then makes an immediate forced move Medium Straight directly forward if in current Gear 1 to 4, or long Straight Forwards if in current Gear 5 or 6, during which it ignores all terrain and other vehicles. This movement causes a Collision Window. This vehicle then gains 2 Hazard Tokens and 1 Audience Vote.

TUMBLE

The vehicle stops at the edge of the Ramp and then makes an immediate additional forced move Short Straight forward, during which it ignores all terrain and other vehicles. This movement causes a Collision Window. This vehicle then suffers a 4D6 attack and gains +6 Hazard Tokens.

If, by ignoring obstructions during a Jump or Tumble, this vehicle's Final Position would overlap an obstruction, move this vehicle backwards along the movement template by the minimum amount to avoid overlapping any obstruction.

AUDIENCE VOTES

Gaslands is a televised death-sport and the organisers want to ensure that the audience stays on the edge of their seats. In recent years, the producers have started to introduce ways for the viewers at home to participate in the carnage. This is represented by Audience Votes.

As you'll see, Audience Votes are used as a positive in-game handicap system, to allow players to get back into the game or to cause general mayhem.

GAINING AUDIENCE VOTES

Players gain Audience Votes when certain conditions are met. The player, not any specific vehicle, gains Audience Votes. A player may have any number of Audience Votes.

AUDIENCE VOTES TABLE	
Condition	**Audience Votes**
A player has one of their vehicles Wrecked	Gain 1 Audience Vote
A player starts a round without any active vehicles	Gain 2 Audience Votes

Each Sponsor also provides teams with additional conditions to gain Audience Votes which reward actions that that sponsor's fans want to see on their TV, as do some scenarios.

Use tokens, dice, gems, or bottle caps to track of how many Audience Votes each player has.

SPENDING AUDIENCE VOTES

When a player has a chance to activate a vehicle, before the player declares which vehicle he or she is going to activate or is forced to pass, the player may announce that they are spending Audience Votes. A player may use Audience Votes in this way even if they have no qualifying vehicles.

Importantly, this means that if it is your turn to activate a vehicle, but you have no qualifying vehicles, you still get a single opportunity to spend Audience Votes before you pass, which can then cause you to have a qualifying vehicle to activate.

In addition, this means that when a Gear Phase begins, if no vehicles currently qualify for an activation in this Gear Phase, each player still gets one chance to spend votes before they are forced to pass.

AUDIENCE VOTE EFFECTS

When a player has an opportunity to spend Audience Votes, that player may spend any number of Audience Votes to declare any number of effects.

BURN RUBBER (1 AUDIENCE VOTE)

Select any vehicle you control. That vehicle may immediately change Gear, either one up or one down, gaining 1 Hazard Token as normal. Use of this effect can allow you to declare an activation with a vehicle that was previously unable to activate in this Gear Phase.

THUNDEROUS APPLAUSE (1 AUDIENCE VOTE)

Select a vehicle you control. Immediately remove D6 Hazard Tokens from that vehicle.

EXECUTIVE INTERVENTION (2 AUDIENCE VOTES)

Select a vehicle you do not control. The selected vehicle immediately gains Hazard Tokens until it has 5 Hazard Tokens.

RELOAD (2 AUDIENCE VOTES)

Select a single weapon or upgrade on a vehicle you control. The selected weapon or upgrade immediately gains 1 Ammo Token.

CARPE DIEM (2 AUDIENCE VOTES)

Immediately move Pole Position to a player of your choice or prevent Pole Position from moving the next time it would be moved.

RESPAWN (3 AUDIENCE VOTES)

You may only use this effect if you have no vehicles currently in play. Select a vehicle that you controlled that has been Wrecked during this game and respawn it. The vehicle regains Hull Points equal to half its Hull Value, rounded down. When respawning a vehicle that is still in play as a wreck, turn its wreck back over to become a vehicle. When respawning a vehicle that is not currently in play, follow the rules given in the scenario.

SPONSORS

With the promise of the right to ascend to the shining Martian pleasure domes, there are many who are ready to generously sponsor new teams. Each sponsor has lucrative advertising deals in place, of course.

A team may choose a Sponsor. This Sponsor immediately grants the team all of the Sponsored Perks for that Sponsor. The choice of Sponsor determines what perks classes this team may purchase from.

RUTHERFORD

Grant Rutherford is the son of a militaristic, American, oil baron. He is aggressive, rich, and uncompromising. His beaming face, beneath his trademark cream Stetson, adorns billboard advertisements for his high-quality and high-priced Rutherford brand weaponry. Teams sponsored by Rutherford gain access to military surplus, missile launchers, tanks, helicopters, and as much ammo as they can carry. After his team won in 2016, he was only too happy to kiss the Earth goodbye and now runs his company from his, highly exclusive, Martian office.

- **Perk Classes**: Badass and Military.

Teams sponsored by Rutherford gain the following Sponsored Perks:

- **Military Hardware**: This team may purchase a single Tank. This team may purchase a single Helicopter.
- **Well Stocked**: This vehicle considers any weapon with the ammo 3 special rule to instead have the ammo 4 special rule when purchased.
- **Might Is Right**: This team may not purchase Lightweight vehicles.
- **Televised Carnage**: If this vehicle causes 6 or more hits in a single Attack Step, before Evades, the controller of this vehicle gains 1 Audience Vote.

MIYAZAKI

Yuri Miyazaki grew up in the rubble of Tokyo, fighting her way to the top of the speedway circuit with incredible feats of daring and vehicular agility. She has a small fleet of elite couriers who run jobs for the wealthiest or most desperate clients. It is whispered that she also runs guns for the Pro-Earth Resistance, but no one who spreads that rumour lives long enough to spread it far. Miyazaki's drivers are unsurpassed in their skill and finesse.

- **Perk Classes**: Daring and Precision.

Teams sponsored by Miyazaki gain the following Sponsored Perks:

- **Virtuoso**: The first time this vehicle Pushes It during an activation, this vehicle may Push It without gaining a Hazard Token.
- **Elegance**: Teams sponsored by Miyazaki may not purchase vehicle types with a base Handling Value of 2 or lower.
- **Showing Off**: At the end of this vehicle's activation, if it resolved at least one Spin result, and resolved at least one Slide result, and changed Gear at least once, and did not Wipeout, then this vehicle gains a Showing Off token.
  If a vehicle with a Showing Off token wipes out, that vehicle must discard its Showing Off token.
  At the end of this vehicle's activation, if every in-play vehicle on this team has a Showing Off token, this player discards all Showing Off tokens and gains 1 Audience Vote for each Showing Off token discarded in this way. Discard all Showing Off tokens at the end of the Gear Phase.

MISHKIN

Andre Mishkin is not a natural sportsman. However, the brilliant Russian engineer and inventor proved in 2010 that technology is just as solid an answer as skill or ferocity on the track. From his research and development facility on Mars he continues to send designs for unusual and devastating weapons and sleek, hi-tech vehicles to Earth for field-testing by the teams he sponsors.

- **Perk Classes**: Military and Technology.

Teams sponsored by Mishkin gain the following Sponsored Perks:

- **Thumpermonkey:** This team may purchase electrical weapons and upgrades.
- **Dynamo:** After activating in Gear Phase 4, 5, or 6, this vehicle may add +1 Ammo Token to a single electrical weapon or electrical upgrade on that vehicle.
- **All the Toys:** Whenever a vehicle in this team attacks with a named weapon that has not been attacked with by any vehicle during this game yet, that vehicle's controller gains 1 Audience Vote.

IDRIS

Yandi Idris was an addict. From the first time the hot and sweet fumes of a singing petrol engine filled his nose he could find no other joy. He said that the first time he pressed that nitro-oxide button was like touching the face of God. Mystical, irrational, and dangerous, the Cult of Speed spread like wildfire after Idris' meteoric rise during the 2012 Gaslands season. He crossed the final finishing line in a ball of fire and his body was never found. His fanatical followers say that at 201mph you can hear his sonorous voice on the rushing head wind.

- **Perk Classes**: Precision and Speed.

Teams following in Idris' tire tracks gain the following Sponsored Perks:

- **N2O Addict**: This team may purchase the Nitro upgrade at half the listed cost.
- **Speed Demon**: When this vehicle gains Hazard Tokens as a result of the Nitro Booster, this vehicle only gains Hazard Tokens until it has 3 Hazard Tokens, rather than 5 Hazard Tokens.
- **Cult of Speed**: During Gear Phase 1, 2, or 3 if this vehicle selects the Long Straight movement template, including when using the Nitro Booster upgrade, this vehicle's controller gains 1 Audience Vote.
- **Kiss My Asphalt**: This team may not purchase Gyrocopters.

Remember that you can select any template you like (and thus trigger the Cult of Speed rule, but if it is not permitted, the player to your left will get to select your template instead.

SLIME

Slime rules a wild and feral city in the Australian wastes known as Anarchy. Young people crawled out of the wreckage of the scorched earth in their thousands to rally round her ragged banner. The wild-eyed and whooping joyful gangs of Anarchy are led by Slime's henchwomen, the Chooks, who seek fame and adoration from the global Gaslands audience.

- **Perk Classes**: Tuning and Reckless.

Teams sponsored by Slime gain the following Sponsored Perks:

- **Pinball**: If this vehicle is involved in a Collision during its Movement Step in which the point of contact on both vehicles is along their side edges, and this vehicle declares a Smash Attack, then this vehicle may immediately resolve another Movement Step after the current Movement Step.
- **Spiked Fist**: This team counts the Ram upgrade as requiring zero build slots.
- **Live Fast**: During this vehicle's activation, if this vehicle begins the Wipeout Step with more Hazard Tokens than Hull Points, this vehicle's controller gains 1 Audience Vote.

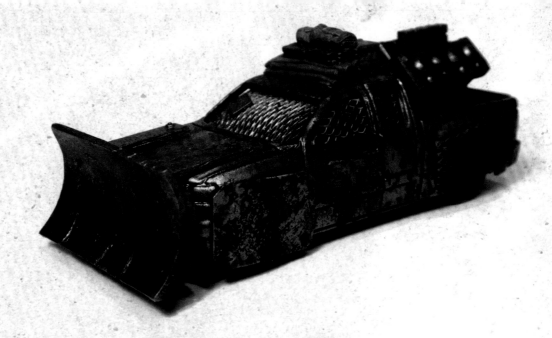

THE WARDEN

Warden Cadeila is proud to live in São Paulo, a shining hub of humanity and relatively untouched by the war. The São Paulo People's Penitentiary has produced three of Gaslands' top ten teams in the past decade, and the Warden continues to grant her prisoners a chance at freedom as long as the Gaslands franchise continues to deliver the sponsorship deals. The deal isn't great for the damned souls who are welded into the Warden's solid steel "coffin cars", but it's better than the alternative.

- **Perks Classes**: Aggression and Badass.

Teams sponsored by the Warden gain the following Sponsored Perks:

- **Prison Cars**: Vehicles in this team may purchase the following upgrade: "**Prison Car:** Reduce the base cost of this vehicle by 4 Cans (to a minimum of 5 Cans). Reduce the Hull Value of this vehicle by 2. May only be purchased by Middleweight vehicles. May only be purchased once for each vehicle.
- **Fireworks**: If this vehicle Explodes, its controller gains 1 Audience Vote if it was Middleweight or 2 Audience Votes if it was Heavyweight, in addition to any votes gained for it being Wrecked. Then discard all Ammo Tokens from the wreck.

SCARLETT

Gaslands is able to support a vast ecosystem of villainous and scurvy raiders, picking off richer teams as their rigs roll from one televised race to the next. Many of these self-styled pirate crews have gained renown, but none have rivalled the infamy or showmanship of **Scarlett Annie**. *A dashing and flamboyant buccaneer, her cult following is likely more to do with her canny association with the long-running "Death Valley Death Run" documentary TV series than any particular skill at dust bowl piracy.*

- **Perk Classes**: Tuning and Aggression.

Teams throwing their lot in with Scarlett gain the following Sponsored Perks:

- **Crew Quarters**: This team may purchase the Extra Crewmember upgrade at half the listed cost.
- **Raiders**: At the end of the Attack Step, this vehicle may permanently reduce its Crew Value by any number, to a minimum of 0 crew. Remove 1 Hull Point from any vehicle in base contact for each crew removed in this way.
- **Raise the Sails**: After rolling Skid Dice, this vehicle may permanently reduce its Crew Value by 1, to a minimum of 0 crew to add 1 free Shift result to the Skid Dice result.
- **Press Gang or Keelhaul:** When another vehicle in contact with this vehicle is Wrecked, this vehicle may either gain 1 crew or gain 2 Audience Votes.

© Sven Siewert

HIGHWAY PATROL

*Along the wrecked and broken highways, where law is another word for vengeance, and justice is a forgotten memory; a handful of souls still cling to a dream of order. Perhaps they do it for the glory. Maybe they even get a kick out of it. They are unsanctioned, unloved and unpaid. Their only power: a badge of bronze. Their only weapon: 600 horsepower of fuel-injected steel. The **Highway Patrol** are the last law in a world gone crazy.*

- **Perk Classes**: Speed and Pursuit.

Teams sponsored by Highway Patrol gain the following Sponsored Perks:

- **Hot Pursuit**: Before the first Gear Phase of the game, after deployment, this team must nominate one enemy vehicle as the "bogey". If the bogey is Wrecked or disqualified, immediately nominate another enemy vehicle to be the bogey.
- **Bogey at 12 o'Clock**: At the end of this vehicle's Movement Step, if the bogey in is this vehicle's front Arc of Fire, and further than Double Range away, and can be seen by this vehicle, this vehicle may immediately resolve another Movement Step.
- **Siren**: At the end of this vehicle's Attack Step, if this vehicle is in the bogey's rear Arc of Fire (regardless of range), the bogey must either reduce its Gear by 1 or gain 2 Hazard Tokens.
- **Steel Justice**: If the bogey wipes out, this team, as a whole, gains 2 Audience Votes. If the bogey is Wrecked this team, as a whole, gains 4 Audience Votes

Teams sponsored by Highway Patrol may purchase the following upgrade:

- **Louder Siren (2 Cans)**: Replace "bogey" with "any enemy vehicle" for the purposes of the Siren special rules.

VERNEY

*Many have taken the bent deal offered by Warden Cadeila but only one has ever earned their freedom. As skilled an engineer as he is a driver, the newly-freed **Verney** now specialised in building unique Frankenstein's monsters of vehicles for anyone who can afford his high-quality customs.*

- **Perk Classes**: Technology and Built.

Teams sponsored by Verney gain the following Sponsored Perks:

- **MicroPlate Armour**: Vehicles in this team may purchase the **MicroPlate Armour** upgrade, which costs 6 Cans, increases the vehicles Hull Value by 2, and requires 0 build slots.
- **Trunk of Junk**: You may attack with any number of dropped weapons in a single activation.
- **Tombstone:** If the shooting template of a shooting attack touches the rear edge of this vehicle, this vehicle gains +1 to its Evade rolls. During this vehicle's Attack Step, this vehicle may gain 2 Hazard Tokens. If it does, all Collisions involving this vehicle are considered to be Head-on until the start of its next activation.
- **That's Entertainment**: Whenever a dropped weapon template that was placed by this team is removed from play, this team gains 1 Audience Vote.

MAXXINE

Maxxine is the current grease-smeared face of The Black Swans. While many might assume art to have been the last thing to survive the Martian bombs, The Black Swans dance their mechanised masque for a hypnotised audience. It's ballet, but the dancers weigh 4,000 pounds and are dripping in engine oil.

- **Perk Classes**: Tuning and Pursuit.

Teams sponsored by Maxxine gain the following Sponsored Perks:

- **Dizzy**: This vehicle may resolve any number of Spin results separately during its Movement Step, one after another. This can allow this vehicle to Spin more than 90 degrees during its Movement Step.
- **Maxximum Drift**: If this vehicle resolves two Slide results in a single Movement Step, it may use the Medium Straight in place of the slide template. If this vehicle resolves three or more Slide results in a single Movement Step, it may use the Long Straight in place of the Slide template.
- **Meshuggah**: When this vehicle resolves a Slide or Spin that ends within Medium range of a friendly vehicle without causing a Collision, this team gains 1 Audience Vote.

THE ORDER OF THE INFERNO

Yandi Idris is not dead. He cannot die. He rides on in the living flame. His voice can be heard in the roar of the road and the screams of superheated metal. Yandi is free, and we can be too. He has shown us the path. Only by knowing the flames can we know true freedom. Buy your copy of "Freedom in The Flames" today to find out more. Available from **Order of the Inferno** *stalls at all major trading outposts.*

- **Perk Classes**: Horror and Speed.

Teams indoctrinated into The Order of the Inferno gain the following Sponsored Perks:

- **Fire Walk With Me**: When this vehicle would receive damage from any weapon or effect with the Fire rule, this vehicle may reduce the damage received by up to three, to a minimum of one.
- **Burning Man**: If this vehicle is On Fire it gains +1 to all Evade dice.
- **Cult of Flame**: At the end of the Gear Phase, if there are more enemy vehicles On Fire than there are friendly vehicles On Fire, or all enemy vehicles are On Fire, this team gains 1 Audience Vote for each friendly vehicle that is On Fire.

BEVERLY, THE DEVIL ON THE HIGHWAY

The low growling of the starting grid was suddenly eclipsed by an ear-splitting, dizzying sound. Eyeball-shakingly loud, the shrill screeching was suffocating. A single car drifted forward into the pack, windows like onyx, bumper corroded. The sound changed timbre, dropping suddenly to a sub-audible throb that tightened chests and shattered headlamps. Despite the harsh desert sun, frost began to form on windshields. **Beverly** *was a stupid story told to scare children. She wasn't real.*

- **Perk classes**: Horror and Built.

Teams haunted by Beverly gain the following Sponsored Perks:

- **Graveyard Shift**: At the start of the game, after deployment, all vehicles in this team except one must gain the Ghost Rider special rule.

- **Ghost Rider:** This vehicle ignores, and is ignored by, other vehicles at all times. This vehicle cannot be involved in Collisions. This vehicle may not make shooting attacks or be attacked with shooting weapons. This vehicle may never count towards the victory conditions of a scenario.
- **Soul Anchor:** If all in-play vehicles from this team have the Ghost Rider special rule immediately remove all vehicles on this team from play.
- **At the Crossroads:** This team may choose to pay only 1 Audience Vote to respawn a vehicle. If they do, the respawned vehicle must gain the Ghost Rider special rule.
- **Inexorable:** If a vehicle from this team is a wreck or out of play, the vehicle may be respawned, even if other rules would ordinarily prevent that.
- **Soul Harvest:** If this vehicle's movement template comes into contact with an enemy vehicle, this vehicle gains 1 Soul Token, even if the enemy vehicle is being ignored. If this vehicle's movement template comes into contact with a friendly vehicle without the Ghost Rider rule that it did not start in contact with, choose one: either gain 1 Audience Vote for each Soul token or repair two Hull Points on the vehicle without the Ghost Rider rule for each Soul Token. Then discard all Soul Tokens from this vehicle.

A Ghost Rider may gain a Soul Token and give it to a friendly vehicle in the same activation, as long as it would come into contact with the enemy vehicle first.

RUSTY'S BOOTLEGGERS

Zeke Rusty and his boys been wall to wall and treetop-tall since before the world went to hell, running moonshine past Smokey back since before the big red one fell. Their stills are volatile, their delivery vehicles are ramshackle, but they still run liquor that grandpappy would be proud of... though none the boys can remember just how he liked it right now. Damn that gin.

- **Perk class**: Reckless and Built.

Teams rum-running for Rusty gain the following Sponsored Perks:

- **Party Hard**: At the end of this vehicle's Attack Step, if this vehicle has more Hazard Tokens than the sum of the Hazard Tokens on all other enemy vehicles within Medium range combined, this vehicle's controller gains 1 Audience Vote for each enemy vehicle with one or more Hazard Tokens within Medium range of this vehicle.
- **Dutch courage**: Vehicles in this team only Wipeout when they have 8 Hazard Tokens.
- **As Straight as I'm Able**: This vehicle does not gain a Hazard Token from the articulated rule if it selects a template that is not a Straight.
- **Over the Limit**: This vehicle never considers any of the Straight movement templates to be permitted. This vehicle considers Veer to be permitted and Trivial in any Gear.
- **Trailer Trash**: This team may purchase Trailers. This team must contain either: one or more Medium or Heavyweight vehicles equipped with a trailer upgrade, or a War Rig.
- **Haulage:** Each vehicle on this team equipped with a trailer upgrade, and each War Rig on this team, may equip a single trailer cargo upgrade for free.

TRAILERS

A trailer is an upgrade. A vehicle may be equipped with a single trailer. A War Rig may not be equipped with the trailer upgrade. A vehicle equipped with a trailer gains the Articulated, Ponderous, and Piledriver special rules, (see War Rig, page 116)

- **Stowage:** Middleweight trailers provide 1 additional build slot to the towing vehicle. Heavyweight trailers provide 3 additional build slots to the towing vehicle. When purchasing a weapon for a vehicle with a trailer, the player must declare whether that weapons is installed on the cab or the trailer. When measuring range, place the shooting template touching either the cab or the trailer, depending on where the weapon is mounted, as per the Articulated rules (see War Rig, page 118).

TRAILER CARGO

Where indicated, a vehicle equipped with a trailer upgrade, or War Rig, may equip a single trailer cargo upgrade.

- **Peach Moonshine:** This vehicle's Molotov Cocktails count as having an infinite number of Ammo Tokens.
- **Sourmash Jet Booster:** At the end of this vehicle's Movement Step, if this vehicle has 5 or more Hazard Tokens, it must immediately make a forced move Long Straight directly forward. This ignores Over the Limit special rule.
- **Siphon Pump:** At the start of this vehicle's Attack Step, regardless of whether it is Distracted, this vehicle may take up to one Hazard Token from each vehicle within Short range of it and place it on this vehicle.
- **Old Fashioned Corn Liquor:** Whenever a vehicle within Medium range of this vehicle gains one or more Hazard Tokens, it gains one additional Hazard Token.
- **Cattle-Hammer:** This vehicle may consider its current Gear to be any value, up to this vehicle's max Gear, during the Wipeout Step, including during any Collisions resolved during the Wipeout Step.

TRAILER UPGRADE TABLE			
Upgrades	**Special Rules**	**Build Slots**	**Cost**
Trailer (Lightweight)	Trailer. Restricted. Stowage.	-	4
Trailer (Middleweight)	Trailer. May only be purchased for middleweight and heavyweight vehicles. Restricted. Stowage.	(+1)	8
Trailer (Heavyweight)	Trailer. May only be purchased for heavyweight vehicles. Restricted. Stowage.	(+3)	12

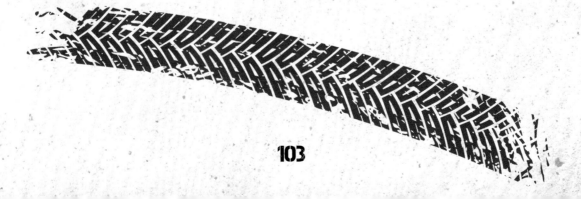

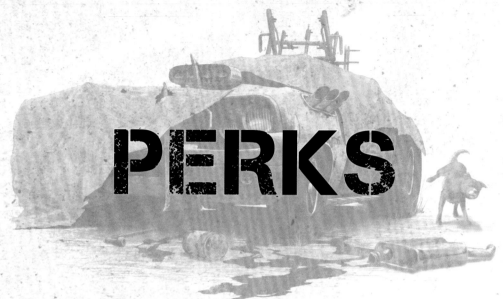

PERKS

Perks represent the skills and experience of the members of your team and allow you to further personalise your team. They are divided into a set of perk classes. Vehicles may only purchase perks from those perks classes lists under their chosen sponsor.

There is no limit to the number of perks each vehicle can have. Each perk may only be purchased once for each vehicle.

AGGRESSION

DOUBLE-BARRELED (2 CANS)

During this vehicle's Attack Step, up to three weapons with the Crew Fired special rule may gain a +1 bonus to hit.

BOARDING PARTY (2 CANS)

This vehicle ignores the Distracted rule, meaning this vehicle may attack during the Attack Step even if the vehicle is touching an obstacle.

BATTLEHAMMER (4 CANS)

When making a Smash Attack, this vehicle gains +1 attack die for each Hazard Token it currently has.

TERRIFYING LUNATIC (5 CANS)

Whenever a vehicle controlled by another player ends its Movement Step within Short range of this vehicle, the active vehicle gains a Hazard Token.

GRINDERMAN (5 CANS)

Before this vehicle rolls its attack dice in a Smash Attack, it may choose to add 1 Hazard Token to the target vehicle for each point of damage it inflicts, instead of removing Hull Points.

MURDER TRACTOR (5 CANS)

This vehicle may make piledriver attacks, like a War Rig.

BADASS

POWDER KEG (1 CAN)

This vehicle may add 1 to its explosion check. Treat this vehicle as one weight-class heavier when it explodes. This bonus **does** apply during resolution of the Fireworks perk.

CROWD PLEASER (1 CAN)

If this vehicle wipes out, gain 1 Audience Vote.

ROAD WARRIOR (2 CANS)

Once per activation, if this vehicle has successfully caused one or more hits on an enemy vehicle at any point during this activation, this vehicle may remove a single Hazard Token at the end of its Attack Step.

COVER ME (2 CANS)

Once during its activation, this vehicle may remove a Hazard Token and place it on another friendly vehicle within Double range.

MADMAN (3 CANS)

At the end of this vehicle's Movement Step, if it has 4 or more Hazard Tokens, it may remove a Hazard Token and place it on another vehicle within Medium range.

BULLET-TIME (3 CANS)

If this vehicle resolves a Slide result during its Movement Step, this may select one of its weapons to count as Turret-mounted for the rest of the activation.

© Jake Zettelmaier

BUILT

DEAD WEIGHT (2 CANS)

During this vehicle's Attack Step, this vehicle may gain 2 Hazard Tokens to count as one weight-class heavier (unless already Heavyweight) until the start of its next activation.

BARREL ROLL (2 CANS)

When this vehicle suffers a Flip, it may choose to place the Flip template touching the centre of either side edge or the rear edge of this vehicle, and perpendicular to that edge, instead of touching the front edge as normal.

BRUISER (4 CANS)

In a Collision involving this vehicle, if this vehicle declares a reaction other than Evade against an enemy vehicle, the enemy vehicle immediately gains one Hazard Token.

SPLASHBACK (5 CANS)

Once per step, when this vehicle loses one or more Hull Points, make a 1D6 attack against each vehicle within Medium range at end of that step.

CRUSHER (7 CANS)

This vehicle gains the Up and Over special rule (See the Monster Truck rules, page 71).

FEEL NO PAIN (8 CANS)

During an enemy vehicle's Attack Step, after an attacker has rolled all their attack dice against this vehicle, if the attacks caused a total of 2 or fewer uncancelled hits, cancel all remaining hits.

DARING

CHROME-WHISPERER (2 CANS)

This vehicle may Push It any number of times during a single Movement Step, gaining 1 Hazard Token each time.

SLIPPERY (3 CANS)

Vehicles making a Smash Attack targeting this vehicle suffer a penalty of -2 attack dice.

HANDBRAKE ARTIST (3 CANS)

When applying a Spin result, this vehicle may choose to face **any** direction.

EVASIVE (5 CANS)

Before making an Evade roll, this vehicle may gain any number of Hazard Tokens to add +1 to each of their Evade dice for each Hazard Token gained. A roll of a "1" on an Evade dice always counts as a failure.

POWERSLIDE (5 CANS)

This vehicle may use any template except the long straight template instead of the slide template when applying a slide result. As with the step 1.1 of Movement Step, you must use the first movement template you touch. Treat the selected movement template as a slide template for purposes of finding the vehicle's Final Position.

STUNT DRIVER (7 CANS)

This perk may only be taken on a lightweight or middleweight vehicle type with a base Handling Value of 3 or more. This vehicle may choose to ignore any number of obstructions during its Movement Step. After any Movement Step in which this vehicle chose to ignore any obstruction using this ability, this vehicle immediately gains 3 Hazard Tokens.

HORROR

PURIFYING FLAMES (1 CAN)

Once per activation, at the start of this vehicle's activation, this vehicle may suffer up to three damage to select any friendly vehicle. For each point of damage suffered via this effect, repair that number of Hull Points on the target vehicle. This damage may not be reduced. This damage counts as having the Fire rule. This effect may not be used to raise a vehicle above its starting Hull Value.

ECSTATIC VISIONS (1 CAN)

Once per activation, at the start of this vehicle's activation, this vehicle may gain up to 3 Hazard Tokens to discard 1 Hazard Token from a friendly vehicle for each Hazard Token gained.

SYMPATHY FOR THE DEVIL (1 CAN)

When this vehicle makes an Evade check, its controller may select a friendly vehicle within Medium range. Add the current Gear of the selected vehicle to this vehicle's current Gear for the purposes of this evade check. Both the selected vehicle and this vehicle suffer any unsaved damage from this attack, including any additional effects.

HIGHWAY TO HELL (2 CANS)

At the end of its Movement Step, if this vehicle selected a straight template, this vehicle may suffer two damage. This damage counts as having the Fire rule. If any Hull Points are removed by this effect, this vehicle may leave its movement template (ignoring any slide template) in play as a Napalm dropped weapon template. Remove this template at the start of this vehicle's next activation. *(You may wish to download and print out extra paper templates for this effect.)*

VIOLENT MANIFESTATION (3 CANS)

When this vehicle is respawned: make an immediate attack (with attack dice based on the weight of the respawned vehicle) against every other vehicle within Medium range as if this vehicle was an exploding wreck. This explosion counts as having both the "Blast" and "Fire" rules.

ANGEL OF DEATH (4 CANS)

Before making an attack, this vehicle may suffer up to three damage to add that many attack dice to a single weapon used in this attack.

MILITARY

DEAD-EYE (2 CANS)

During this vehicle's Attack Step, this vehicle gains +1 bonus to hit if making a shooting attack at a target within Double range and not within Medium range. Critical Hits still occur only on the natural roll of a 6.

LOADER (2 CANS)

At the start of its Attack Step, this vehicle may temporarily reduce its Crew Value by one, once, until the end of the Attack Step, to gain +1 bonus to hit with a single weapon. Critical Hits still occur only on the natural roll of a 6.

FULLY LOADED (2 CANS)

If a shooting weapon on this vehicle has 3 or more Ammo Tokens remaining before discarding an Ammo Token to attack, that weapon gains +1 attack die.

RAPID FIRE (2 CANS)

Once per round, after attacking with a weapon, this vehicle may resolve an additional Attack Step in which it may only attack with that weapon.

HEADSHOT (4 CANS)

When making a shooting attack, this vehicle's Critical Hits inflict 3 hits instead of the normal two hits.

RETURN FIRE (5 CANS)

Once per Gear Phase, if this vehicle is the target of a shooting attack, this vehicle may take 2 Hazard Tokens to immediately attack, as if it was this vehicle's Attack Step.

PRECISION

MISTER FAHRENHEIT (2 CANS)

This vehicle cannot gain more than 2 Hazard Tokens from Collisions during a single activation.

MOMENT OF GLORY (2 CANS)

Once per game, after rolling the Skid Dice, but before resolving the results, this vehicle may immediately change any number of Skid Dice to any results they choose.

RESTRAINT (2 CANS)

When this vehicle would gain a Hazard Token for shifting **down** a Gear, this vehicle may remove one Hazard Token instead.

EXPERTISE (3 CANS)

This vehicle adds 1 to its Handling Value.

TRICK DRIVING (3 CANS)

This vehicle may select a movement template as if its current Gear was one higher or one lower.

EASY RIDER (5 CANS)

Once per round, this vehicle may discard one rolled Skid Dice result before applying the results.

PURSUIT

ON YOUR TAIL (2 CANS)

When an enemy vehicle resolves a Spin or Slide move that ends within Short range of this vehicle, that enemy vehicle gains 1 Hazard Token.

SCHADENFREUDE (2 CANS)

If another vehicle wipes out within Short range of this vehicle, (either before or after any Flip), remove all Hazard Tokens from this vehicle.

TAUNT (2 CANS)

At the start of this vehicle's Attack Step, roll a Skid Die. If you roll something other than a Shift result, you may place that Skid Dice result onto the dashboard of a target vehicle within Short range. This Skid Dice result must be resolved during that vehicle's next Movement Step, and may not be re-rolled.

OUT RUN (2 CANS)

At the start of this vehicle's Attack Step, all vehicles within Short range of this vehicle and in a lower current Gear than this vehicle gains 1 Hazard Token.

PIT (4 CANS)

During this vehicle's activation, if this vehicle is involved in a non-head-on Collision with an enemy vehicle, it may declare a "Pursuit Intervention Technique" (PIT) as its reaction, targeting the enemy vehicle, instead of declaring a Smash Attack or an Evade. If this vehicle declares a PIT, it may select any movement template the target vehicle considers Hazardous in its current Gear. Immediately after the resolution of this Collision, the target vehicle must make a forced move directly forward using the selected movement template.

UNNERVING EYE CONTACT (5 CANS)

Enemy vehicles within Short range of this vehicle may not use Shift results to remove Hazard Tokens from their dashboard.

RECKLESS

DRIVE ANGRY (1 CAN)

At the start of this vehicle's activation, this vehicle gains 1 Hazard Token.

HOG WILD (2 CANS)

During a Collision resolved during a Wipeout Step, this vehicle gains +2 Smash Attack dice.

IN FOR A PENNY (2 CANS)

If this vehicle has gained six or more Hazard Tokens during this activation, it may double the attack dice of any Smash Attack it makes for the remainder of this activation.

DON'T COME KNOCKING (4 CANS)

At the start of this vehicle's activation, it may gain 4 Hazard Tokens. If it does, this vehicle cannot gain or lose any Hazard Tokens by any means until the start of its next activation.

BIGGER'N YOU (4 CANS)

If this vehicle is involved in a Collision, double any Smash Attack bonuses or penalties resulting from weight differences during that Collision.

BEERSERKER (5 CANS)

When this vehicle would suffer damage outside of its activation, reduce that damage by 1, to a minimum of 1.

SPEED

HOT START (1 CAN)

Roll a D6 at the start of the game. This vehicle starts the game in that Gear. Re-roll if this would put the current Gear of the vehicle above its max Gear.

SLIPSTREAM (2 CANS)

If this vehicle is involved in a tailgate Collision during its activation, this vehicle may declare a Slipstream reaction. If they do, the other vehicle may not declare a reaction. If this vehicle declares a Slipstream reaction, this vehicle may change up or down one Gear and gains a Hazard Token. Neither vehicle gains Hazard Tokens as a result of this Collision.

OVERLOAD (2 CANS)

When resolving Skid Dice during the Movement Step, this vehicle may roll one additional Skid Die. If it does, it must change up at least one Gear or gain a Hazard Token.

DOWNSHIFT (3 CANS)

At the end of a Movement Step in which this vehicle changed down one or more Gears, this vehicle may make a forced move Short Straight forward.

TIME EXTENDED! (3 CANS)

At the end of a Movement Step in which this vehicle passes a race gate, this vehicle may remove any number of Hazard Tokens.

HELL FOR LEATHER (5 CANS)

This vehicle considers Long Straight to be permitted in any Gear. The Long Straight is not considered either Hazardous or Trivial in any Gear.

TECHNOLOGY

ROCKET THRUSTERS (1 CAN)

When this vehicle is moved as part of a Flip, it may choose to use the Long Straight, Veer, or Gentle templates instead of the Medium Straight template.

WHIZBANG (1 CAN)

At the start of each game, this vehicle gains a random Speed perk. This perk is lost at the end of the game.

GYROSCOPE (1 CAN)

At the start of each game, this vehicle gains a random Daring perk. This perk is lost at the end of the game.

SATELLITE NAVIGATION (2 CANS)

When this vehicle resolves its Skid Dice, this vehicle's controller may set aside one Shift result. This vehicle may have any number of Shift results set aside. Any vehicle in this team may use these set aside Shift results during a later Movement Step, as if they had rolled them in that Movement Step.

MOBILE MECHANIC (3 CANS)

Once per activation, at the start of its Attack Step, this vehicle may temporarily reduce its Crew Value by one, once, until the end of the Attack Step, to perform a field repair. If it does, this vehicle gains 1 Hull Point, which may not take its Hull Points above the vehicle's Hull Value.

EUREKA! (4 CANS)

Once per game, at the start of its Attack Step, this vehicle's controller may declare any weapon that this vehicle has not attacked with yet this game. This vehicle counts as being armed with the declared weapon, on a facing of their choice, for the next attack only.

TUNING

FENDERKISS (2 CANS)

When this vehicle makes a Smash Attack, this vehicle suffers a penalty of -2 attack dice. Vehicles making a Smash Attack targeting this vehicle suffer a penalty of -2 attack dice.

REAR DRIVE (2 CANS)

This vehicle may pivot about the centre of its front edge, rather than the centre of the vehicle, when resolving Spin results.

DELICATE TOUCH (3 CANS)

This vehicle ignores the hazard icons on movement templates.

MOMENTUM (3 CANS)

When resolving Skid Dice, this vehicle may set aside a Slide or Spin result to re-roll a Skid Dice. This effect may be used multiple times. Skid Dice that are set aside must be resolved.

PURRING (6 CANS)

This vehicle does not gain more than 1 Hazard Token from Spin results each activation. This vehicle does not gain more than 1 Hazard Token from Slide results each activation. This vehicle does not gain more than 1 Hazard Token from Hazard results each activation.

SKIING (6 CANS)

If this vehicle has Handling 3 or higher, this vehicle may take 3 Hazard Tokens at the end of its Movement Step to be ignored by other vehicles during their Movement Steps until the start of this vehicle's next activation. If, by ignoring this vehicle in this way, a vehicle's Final Position would overlap it, move that vehicle backwards along their movement template by the minimum amount to avoid overlapping any obstruction.

THE WAR RIG

The War Rig is a massive vehicle and behaves in a couple of unique ways on the tabletop. It has the Articulated, Ponderous, and Piledriver special rules.

MODELLING YOUR WAR RIG

As you will see the rules surrounding the War Rig require you to treat the cab and the trailer as somewhat separate game elements.

Because of this, it is highly recommended that you model your War Rig in such a way that the cab and trailer can be separated and hinged during play. You might choose to use small magnets, a pin, or peg to connect the two halves while allowing them to be separated and hinged during play.

ARTICULATED

CAB AND TRAILER

An articulated vehicle is comprised of two parts: the cab and the trailer. The front part of the articulated vehicle is referred to as the cab. The rear part of the articulated vehicle is referred to as the trailer. The cab and trailer are connected by a hitch.

ARMING AN ARTICULATED VEHICLE

When arming an articulated vehicle with a weapon, the player must declare whether that weapon is mounted on the cab or the trailer. When measuring range, place the shooting template touching either the cab or the trailer, depending on where the weapon is mounted.

ARTICULATED MOVEMENT

When moving an articulated vehicle, the cab is moved like a normal vehicle, separately to the trailer, and then the trailer is place back into contact with the cab once it is in its Final Position.

To move an articulated vehicle, follow these steps:

- Select a movement template as normal
- If the vehicle selects any template other than a Straight, it gains 1 Hazard Token
- Place the movement template so that it is touching the centre of the front edge of the cab
- Optionally, roll and resolve Skid Dice as normal
- Ignoring the trailer, place the cab in its Final Position
- Place the trailer so that it is reconnected with the hitch of the cab, covering as much of the surface area of the movement template as possible.

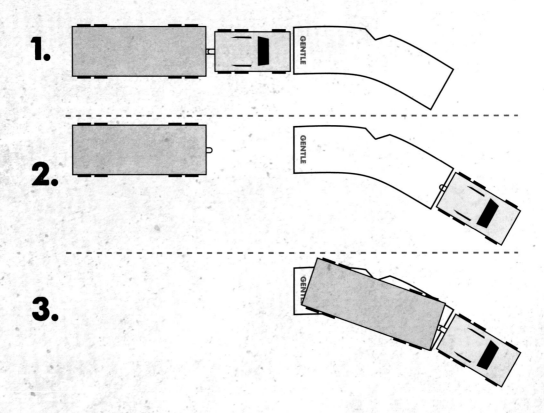

The trailer should follow the path of the cab as closely as possible during this vehicle's movement. This is enforced by ensuring that the trailer is covering as much of the surface area of the movement template as possible, but sometimes a little player judgement may be needed to ensure it moves in a way that you feel is realistic.

BACK HER UP

When a War Rig is moving in reverse, treat the rear of the trailer as the front of the cab, and treat the cab as the trailer.

PIVOTING AN ARTICULATED VEHICLE

When pivoting an articulated vehicle, for example when resolving a Spin, pivot both cab and trailer together as a single fixed object around its shared centre point.

JACKKNIFE

If an articulated vehicle suffers a Flip, do not resolved a Flip and instead resolve a Jackknife:

- **Swing Trailer:** The player to the left hinges the trailer into any position they like, without disconnecting or overlapping the cab and trailer. This creates a COLLISION WINDOW.
- **Pivot Vehicle:** The player to the left then pivots the articulated vehicle to face any direction. This creates a COLLISION WINDOW.
- **Crunch:** The articulated vehicle than performs a 4D6 attack against itself that cannot be Evaded.

PONDEROUS

Ponderous vehicles are inexorable, unable to manoeuvre easily but also hard to shift from their current course once they are rolling.

TANKER ANCHOR

At the start of its activation, a Ponderous vehicle may gain 1 Hazard Token to skip its Movement Step. The massive vehicle may then increase its current Gear by 1.

SLIDES

When a Ponderous vehicle resolves a Slide result, it must ignore the Slide template: do not place it. Each Slide result provides a Hazard Token as normal.

WIPEOUTS

When a Ponderous vehicle suffers a Wipeout, the player to the left does not pivot it during the final step of the Wipeout process. Leave it in its current orientation.

WAR RIG WIPEOUT

When a War Rig suffers a Wipeout, a failed Flip check results in a Jackknife, rather than a Flip (because it is Articulated), and it doesn't get pivoted at the end of the Wipeout (because it is Ponderous).

© Jake Zettelmaier

PILEDRIVER ATTACK

During this vehicle's Movement Step, when this vehicle collides with another vehicle of a lighter weight-class, it may declare a Piledriver Attack as its reaction. A Piledriver Attack counts as a Smash Attack in all regards, and also includes an additional effect.

If a vehicle is targeted with a Piledriver Attack, after resolving the Collision, the controller of the vehicle that made the Piledriver Attack may place the target vehicle anywhere within Short range of the target vehicle's original position, then pivot the target vehicle to face any direction, such that it does not collide with the active vehicle again during this Movement Step.

If the War Rig has a Ram on the appropriate facing, the piledriver attack does benefit from the Ram's special rules.

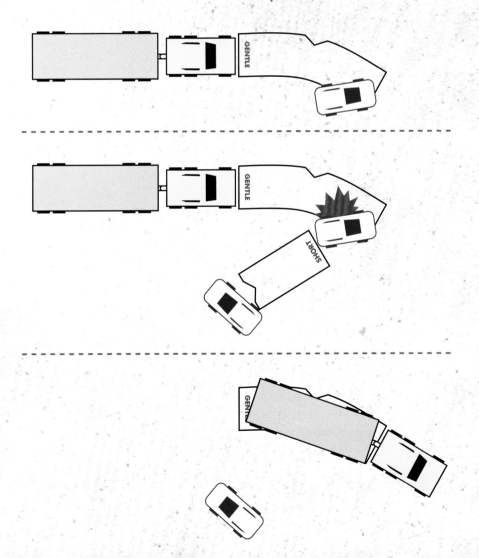

WAYS TO PLAY

In this section you will find a number of different ways to play *Gaslands*. The first is the Death Race. After this, there are a selection of other scenarios, which provide new game modes to enjoy. This section also includes some rules for basic campaigns, plus a set of rules for running more advanced campaigns, called "Televised Seasons". Finally, this section contains a narrative campaign that centres around the War Rig, to allow you play the classic "defend the rig" genre experience!

SCENARIOS

There are a great many ways to play *Gaslands*. Feel free to choose a scenario or roll a D6 on any of these tables to generate a scenario at random:

TELEVISED EVENT SCENARIO TABLE	
D6 Roll	Scenario
1–2	Death Race
3	Arena of Death
4	Capture the Flag
5	Flag Tag
6	Saturday Night Live

WASTELAND SKIRMISH SCENARIO TABLE	
D6 Roll	**Scenario**
1	Automated Salvage
2	Express Delivery
3–4	Scavenger Party
5	The Revolution Will Be Televised
6	Zombie Bash

SPECIAL EVENT SCENARIO TABLE	
D6	**Scenario**
1	Big Game Hunter
2	Desert Strike
3–4	Monster Truck Smash
5	Tank Commander
6	Truckasaurus

TEAM GAMES

Gaslands is great played as a team game. For example, Death Races work great with up to four teams of two players, each with a single vehicle.

When playing team games, here are some additional rules:

- A player may never pass Pole Position to a teammate. Instead, they must pass it to the next eligible player that is not on the same team.
- When resolving a Wipeout, a player may never pivot a teammate's vehicle. Instead, the next player around the table that is not on the same team must pivot the vehicle.
- Player's may not "premeasure" movement templates for teammates. This will count as the player herself touching the template.
- When a player has an opportunity to spend Audience Votes, that player may consider all vehicles on the same team as them as if they were vehicles that they control for the purposes of spending Audience Votes.
- Replace "player" with "team" for scenario victory conditions.

DEATH RACE

"Through the shimmering haze of the broken, steaming asphalt, we see our steel-eyed competitors lined up, with engines rattling and teeth gritted. Tonight's race is incredibly important to the teams… it's the last chance for a shot in the big leagues next month, and one more crucial step on that road to The Big Red."

In a Death Race, participates must race through the gates in the right order, in the right direction, faster than the other guys, or be the last wheels rolling.

RACE GATES

A Gate is formed by placing two small obstacles exactly long straight apart. Gates have an orientation and there is only one correct way through a gate. Gates are numbered. The invisible line between the centre-points of the two objects forms the line of the Gate.

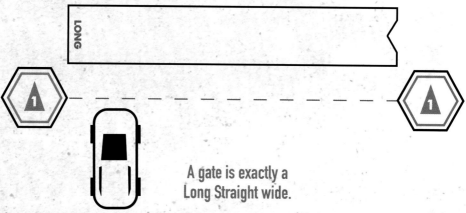

A gate is exactly a
Long Straight wide.

The two objects that make up the Gate's edges count as Middleweight obstacles, but the gap between the obstacles counts as an open surface. Alternatively, use a flat template the same dimensions as the Long Straight template as the gate, and treat it as an open surface.

SETUP
RACE TRACK

Set up three or more Gates at least one Long Straight away from each other. Orient the Gates as you choose. Choose any one of the Gates to be the Starting Line and another Gate to be the Finish Line, (or one Gate to represent both if the track is a loop) or a figure of eight. Then lay out some terrain to represent a post-apocalyptic death race.

There are a great number of possible racetrack layouts. To create a fun track, keep in mind a couple of general guidelines:

- Try to ensure Gates are no more than 3 x Long Straight distance apart
- Ensure there are plenty of obstacles actually on the track and in the way of the race
- If possible, ensure that race leaders are forced to come back into contact with race laggards (a figure of 8 layout is great for this, as is a teardrop shape). This keeps the late game interesting.
- Keep the run from the starting line to Gate 1 reasonable clear of obstructions and an easy drive.

Here is an example setup, using four gates, that will provide a "figure of eight" race track.

Here is an example setup, using three gates, that will provide a "tear-drop" race track.

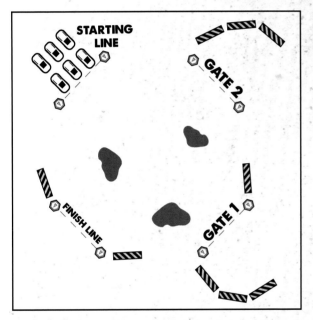

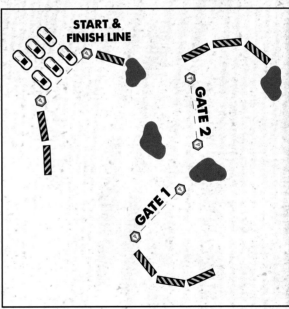

///// Barriers   ⬡ Gates   ● Rubble

POLE POSITION

Roll off to determine who has Pole Position. The player with Pole Position deploys the first vehicle and activates the first vehicle in each Gear Phase.

Whenever the player with Pole Position passes a Gate with any vehicle, excluding the Starting Line, they must immediately choose another player and pass Pole Position to them.

STARTING GRID

The race begins on the Starting Line. Behind the starting line is the Starting Grid. The Starting Grid is a grid as wide as the number of players and as deep as required to deploy all vehicles.

Starting with the player in Pole Position, players take it in turns to place a vehicle anywhere in the first rank of the Starting Grid, touching the Starting Line. Players must fill up the first rank of the Starting Grid before a vehicle can be placed into the second rank, and so on.

STARTING LINE

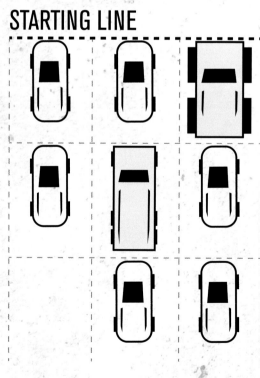

Vehicles must be placed into the Starting Grid such that they are not touching any other vehicle. Vehicles must be placed leaving a finger's width gap on all sides of the vehicle.

THE RACE

PASSING GATES

When any part of a vehicle touches the line of a Gate, while travelling in the correct direction, it passes that Gate. A vehicle must pass the previous Gate before it can pass the subsequent gate. E.g. a vehicle must pass Gate 2 before it is able to pass Gate 3 and so on.

GREEN LIGHT, GO!

As soon as the game begins, all vehicles count as having passed the starting line automatically and may proceed to Gate 1 immediately. (This rule helps lessen pile-ups on the starting line, although won't prevent them altogether!).

WEAPONS INACTIVE UNTIL GATE 1

Vehicles may not make weapon attacks until they have passed Gate 1 and their weapons activate. Before a vehicle passes Gate 1, all of their weapon systems are disabled, although they are free to make Smash Attacks as part of Collisions. Upgrades can still be used. For the avoidance of doubt, Gate 1 is the first gate after the Starting Line.

CATCH UP MECHANIC

The producers of the Gaslands TV show don't like a clear winner. It doesn't make good television. If you are using Audience Votes, (see page 88), when a vehicle is the **first** to pass any given gate that game, each other player rolls a D6, and adds the number of Gates behind the active vehicle that their front-most vehicle is. If the total is 6 or more, they immediately gain 1 Audience Vote.

Put another way, if you are just one Gate behind, you get an Audience Vote on a roll of a 5+. If your best car is lagging two Gates behind the leader, you get an Audience Vote on a roll of a 4+, and so on.

RESPAWNING

In a Death Race scenario, when a vehicle that is not in play as a wreck is respawned, its controller may place the vehicle so that it is touching the line of the last Gate that it had passed prior to being Wrecked, facing in any direction.

© James Hall

RACE END
FINISH LINE

The Finish Line can be passed only after passing all previous Gates. The finish line may be the final Gate, or it might be the Starting Line again, in the case of a looping track layout.

GAME END

At the end of any Gear Phase, if only one player has vehicles in play, the game ends and that player is the winner.

When the first non-Helicopter, non-Gyrocopter vehicle has passed the finish line the game is over and the controller of that vehicle is the winner.

RUNNERS UP

If you want to find out the order of the runners up, as soon as the first vehicle has passed the finish line, freeze play and check the positions of all vehicles. The vehicle that has passed the finish line is the winner. The closest vehicle to the finish line that has also passed all previous Gates is in second place, and so on.

TELEVISED EVENTS

ARENA OF DEATH

"Tonight's games are a simple affair. You know the rules. I know the rules. The drivers sure as hell know the rules. Well… most of the rules… ACTIVATE THE TURRETS! [Wild applause]"

SETUP

Lay out some terrain to represent a dystopian demolition derby arena.

POLE POSITION

Players roll-off for Pole Position. At the end of each Gear Phase, pass the Pole Position marker clockwise.

DEPLOYMENT

Starting with the player with Pole Position, players take it in turns to place a spawn point, which is a round counter no larger than a penny (20mm), on the table within Medium range of any table edge and more than Double range from any other spawn point. Then, starting with the player with Pole Position, players take it in turns to deploy all of their vehicles within Short range of their spawn point (measured like a shooting attack).

Roll 2D6. This is the number of gun turrets to be deployed. Starting with the player with Pole Position, players (or teams) take it in turn to deploy a gun turret each until all turrets are deployed. When deploying a gun turret, it may be deployed anywhere on the table, not touching a vehicle or terrain.

SPECIAL RULES

Players may not use respawn during this game.

GUN TURRETS

Gun Turrets count as Middleweight Destructible obstacles. They may be targeted with shooting attacks, and have 4 Hull Points if shot at.

Gun turrets automatically make a 2D6 shooting attack targeting the first vehicle to end their Movement Step within Medium range of the turret each Gear Phase. The target may Evade as normal.

VICTORY CONDITIONS

At the end of any Gear Phase, if only one player has vehicles in play, the game ends and that player is the winner.

CAPTURE THE FLAG

"Ladies and Gentlemen in the arena tonight. Online viewers. Sports fans. When two tribes go to war, only Premium Subscribers get FlagCam!"

SETUP

Lay out some terrain to represent a dystopian demolition derby arena.

POLE POSITION

Roll-off for Pole Position. At the end of each Gear Phase, pass the Pole Position marker clockwise.

DEPLOYMENT

Starting with the player with Pole Position, players take it in turns to place a spawn point, which is a round counter no larger than a penny (20mm), on the table within Medium range of any table edge and more than Double range from any other spawn point. Then, starting with the player with Pole Position, players take it in turns to deploy all of their vehicles within Short range of their spawn point (measured like a shooting attack). When using Audience Votes to respawn, a vehicle must respawn within Short range of its controller's spawn point.

After deployment, each player places a flag on one vehicle they control. Place the flag on the vehicle's dashboard.

FLAGS

Flags are lightweight destructible obstacles. To represent a flag on the tabletop use an object or miniature approximately 30mm in diameter or smaller. You might use a crate, token, bottle cap or a literal little flag.

A vehicle may pick up a flag if its movement template or Final Position touches the flag. When picked up, place the flag on the vehicle's dashboard. When a vehicle is Wrecked, the vehicle's owner must place the flag in play, touching the wreck.

At the end of a vehicle's activation, it may place any flag it is carrying within Short range of itself.

GAME END AND VICTORY

The game ends when one vehicle is carrying two flags. The controller of that vehicle is the winner.

FLAG TAG

The time the producers used barrels packed with high explosives in place of the standard rubber flagpoles certainly got the highest ratings, but the organisers can't seem to get the teams to commit to a sequel.

SETUP

Lay out some terrain to represent a dystopian demolition derby arena.

POLE POSITION

Players roll-off for Pole Position. At the end of each Gear Phase, pass the Pole Position marker clockwise.

DEPLOYMENT

Starting with the player with Pole Position, players take it in turns to place a spawn point, which is a round counter no larger than a penny (20mm), on the table within Medium range of any table edge and more than Double range from any other spawn point. Then, starting with the player with Pole Position, players take it in turns to deploy all of their vehicles within Short range of their spawn point (measured in the same way as a shooting attack). When using Audience Votes to respawn, a vehicle must respawn within Short range of its controller's spawn point.

Each player deploys a flag within Medium range of his or her spawn point, and further than Medium range from any table edge.

FLAGS

Flags are Lightweight, Destructible obstacles. To represent a flag on the tabletop, use an object or miniature approximately 30mm in diameter or smaller. You might use a crate, token, bottle cap, or a literal little flag.

If a vehicle collides with another player's flag the controller of that vehicle gains 1 Victory Point. Because the flag is a Destructible obstacle, it is removed after resolving the Collision.

At the start of each Gear Phase, a player that has no flag in play must redeploy their flag within Medium range of their spawn point, and further than Medium range from any table edge.

You could try making the flags Middleweight Volatile obstacles instead!

VICTORY CONDITIONS

The first player to 3 Victory Points is the winner and the game ends.

SATURDAY NIGHT LIVE

"It's the biggest, most explosive night of the week! The teams are arrayed before us, hungry to impress. Because, of course, tonight, YOU decide the winner!"

SETUP

Lay out some terrain to represent a dystopian demolition derby arena.

POLE POSITION

Players roll-off for Pole Position. At the end of each Gear Phase, pass the Pole Position marker clockwise.

DEPLOYMENT

Starting with the player with Pole Position, players take it in turns to place a spawn point, which is a round counter no larger than a penny (20mm), on the table within Medium range of any table edge and more than Double range from any other spawn point. Then, starting with the player with Pole Position, players take it in turns to deploy all of their vehicles within Short range of their spawn point (measured in the same way as a shooting attack). When using Audience Votes to respawn, a vehicle must respawn within Short range of its controller's spawn point.

SPECIAL RULES

- **Screen Time**: A vehicle may only gain Victory Points if they are within Double range of any enemy vehicle at the point that the Victory Points would be gained.
- **Prizes Mean Points**: Whenever a player gains one or more Audience Votes, they also gain an equal number of Victory Points.

SPECIAL PRIZES

Throughout the game, vehicles can win special prizes for entertaining the audience at home.

At the start of the first round, and whenever a special prize is claimed, roll a D6 and add the current Gear Phase number and round number. The result indicates the special prize condition. If the generated special prize is the same as the last active Special Prize, re-roll it until a different special prize is generated. TV audiences have a very short attention span.

Whenever a vehicle or player meets the current special prize conditions, its controller may claim the special prize to gain 1 Audience Vote (and therefore also 1 Victory Point). That player then rolls to generate a new special prize.

A player may not gain two or more Audience Votes from the same Special Prize condition in a single activation.

Check out gaslands.com/snl for an app to track the special prizes.

SPECIAL PRIZES TABLE	
Result	Special Prize Conditions
3	Control the active vehicle.
4	Control the active vehicle when the active vehicle is in current Gear 3 or higher.
5	Control the active vehicle when any part of the active vehicle's movement template or Final Position falls within Short range of the centre point of the table.
6	Control the active vehicle and have Pole Position.
7	Control the active vehicle and discard its last Hazard Token without wiping out.
8	Control the active vehicle and select a Hazardous template.
9	Control the active vehicle and declare a T-Bone Smash Attack.
10	Control the active vehicle when any vehicle within Double range of the active vehicle loses one or more Hull Points.
11	Control the active vehicle when any vehicle within Double range of the active vehicle has 8 or more Hazard Tokens.
12	Control the active vehicle when any vehicle within Double range of the active vehicle fails a Flip check.
13	Control the active vehicle when any vehicle within Double range of the active vehicle is Wrecked.
14	Control the active vehicle when any vehicle within Double range of the active vehicle Explodes.
15+	Control the active vehicle when the active vehicle is in a current Gear equal to its max Gear.

For the avoidance of doubt, the active vehicle is within Double range of itself.

VICTORY CONDITIONS

The first player to possess 15 Victory Points is the winner.

© Sven Siewert

WASTELAND SKIRMISHES

AUTOMATED SALVAGE

"We take whatever isn't nailed down. For the stuff that is, we use the magnetic nail remover."

SETUP

Lay out some terrain to represent a post-apocalyptic wasteland.

POLE POSITION

Roll-off for Pole Position. At the end of each Gear Phase, pass the Pole Position marker clockwise.

DEPLOYMENT

Starting with the player with Pole Position, players take it in turns to place a spawn point, which is a round counter no larger than a penny (20mm), on the table within Medium range of any table edge and more than Double range from any other spawn point. Then, starting with the player with Pole Position, players take it in turns to deploy all of their vehicles within Short range of their spawn point (measured in the same way as a shooting attack). When using audience votes to respawn, a vehicle must respawn within Short range of its controller's spawn point.

SPECIAL RULES

- **Scarper:** Disqualified vehicles do not count as destroyed and may not respawn.
- **Magnetic Scavenger Hooks:** Whenever a vehicle's movement template or Final Position comes within Short range of an enemy vehicle: the active vehicle gains 1 Salvage Point.
- **Ramshackle:** Once per step, if a vehicle suffers damage its controller places 1 Salvage Counter, which is a round counter no larger than a penny (20mm), touching any point on the vehicle's side edge. If a vehicle's final position or move template overlaps a Salvage Counter, it gains 1 Salvage Point and the Salvage Counter is removed from play.
- **Twisted Metal:** If a vehicle is destroyed all its Salvage Points are lost.

GAME END

Game lasts until only one vehicle remains or after three rounds, whichever comes first.

VICTORY CONDITIONS

The player with the most Salvage Points at the end of the game is the winner, including any on vehicles that have scarpered.

SPOILS

If you are playing a Televised Season (see page 156), at the end of the game each player gains a number of Cans equal to the Salvage Points they collected.

EXPRESS DELIVERY

"When it absolutely, positively has to get there on time, it's best to hire a homicidal petrol-head with a minigun and a deathwish."

SETUP

Lay out some terrain to represent a post-apocalyptic wasteland.

POLE POSITION

Roll-off for Pole Position. At the end of each Gear Phase, pass the Pole Position marker clockwise. If a player with Pole Position is the Leader, they must immediately pass Pole Position to the player to their left.

DEPLOYMENT

Nominate one table edge as the entry edge, the opposite table edge becomes the exit edge.

Starting with the player with Pole Position, players take it in turns to place a spawn point, which is a round counter no larger than a penny (20mm), anywhere touching the entry edge and more than Medium range from any other spawn point. Then, starting with the player with Pole Position, players take it in turns to deploy all of their vehicles within Short range of their spawn point (measured like a shooting attack). When using audience votes to respawn, a vehicle must respawn within Short range of its controller's spawn point.

SPECIAL RULES

- **Delivery Slips:** At the start of the game, each player writes their name on a slip of paper. Fold these slips up and hand one out randomly to each player. Players may check their own slips at any time.
- **Exchanging Details:** Whenever vehicles belonging to two different players are involved in a collision, they must swap slips immediately after resolving the collision.
- **Express Delivery:** When the movement template or final position of a vehicle overlaps the exit edge, that vehicle "exits" the current table and its controllers gains 1 Victory Point, up to a maximum of 1 Victory Point per table.

© James Hall

ROLLING ROAD

When the first vehicle exits the table, remove it and it becomes the Leader. Mark the leader and any vehicle that exits the table in the same Gear Phase that the leader exits as "1". Mark vehicles exiting the table in the following Gear Phase (even if this is during the following round) as "2" and so on. Mark the place that each vehicle exits the table (perhaps by just leaving the vehicle on the edge of the table with a die on it to indicate its marked number). All vehicles still in play after the Gear Phase marking vehicles as "6" are disqualified.

When no vehicles are on the table, take it in turns to rearrange the terrain, leaving the spawn points in place. No terrain may be placed within Long range of the entry edge. This counts as a new table.

Start a new round. Deploy all vehicles marked "1" at the start of Gear Phase 1, "2" at the start of Gear Phase 2 and so on. When deploying a vehicle, place it on the point on the entry edge exactly opposite its exit point. These vehicles remain in the same Gear that they exit the table in.

GAME END

Once one player has scored 2 Victory Points, continue play until all vehicles have exited the current table or been disqualified and then end the game.

VICTORY

Once the game ends, the player that first reached 2 Victory Points is the winner.

SPOILS

If you are playing a Televised Season (see page 156), each vehicle that exits the final table earns their team 1D6 Cans during the post-game sequence. Each player gains 1D6 Cans for each Victory Point they scored. Any player that ends the game with 2 Victory Points and their own Delivery Slip gains an additional 4D6 Cans.

SCAVENGER PARTY

A storm overnight has blown back the dust from a previously buried garage, revealing a fuel dump. The teams dash to the location to grab the supplies whilst they last.

SETUP

Lay out some terrain to represent a post-apocalyptic wasteland.

- **Crates**: Take D6+6 crates and place them in a rough circle, with each crate exactly Double range from the centre of the play area. Use tokens or miniatures no larger than 30mm square to represent the crates.

POLE POSITION

Roll-off for Pole Position. At the end of each Gear Phase, pass the Pole Position marker clockwise.

DEPLOYMENT

Starting with the player with Pole Position, players take it in turns to place a spawn point, which is a round counter no larger than a penny (20mm), on the table within Medium range of any table edge and more than Double range from any other spawn point. Then, starting with the player with Pole Position, players take it in turns to deploy all of their vehicles within Short range of their spawn point (measured in the same way as a shooting attack). When using Audience Votes to respawn, a vehicle must respawn within Short range of its controller's spawn point.

SPECIAL RULES

- **Scarper:** Disqualified vehicles do not count as destroyed and may not respawn.
- **Crates**: If the movement template or the final location of a vehicle touches a crate, or you spin or pivot into contact with a crate, that vehicle may pick up that crate. Place the crate on the vehicle's dashboard to indicate this it is holding the crate. When a vehicle is Wrecked, the vehicle's owner must place any held crates touching the wreck. If a vehicle is disqualified, the vehicle's owner keeps the crate, and may count the crate as held at the end of the game.
- **Loot Boxes:** When a vehicle picks up a crate, it gains a bonus item. Roll a die to see what bonus item this vehicle gains:

LOOT BOX TABLE	
D6 Roll	Loot Box
1	This vehicle gains a Nitro Booster with Ammo 1.
2	This vehicle gains an Oil Slick Dropper with Ammo 1.
3	This vehicle gains a Napalm Dropper with Ammo 1.
4	This vehicle gains a turret-mounted Bazooka with Ammo 1.
5	This vehicle gains a turret-mounted Flamethrower with Ammo 1.
6	This vehicle gains turret-mounted Rockets with Ammo 1.

Each of these bonus items require no build slots and may not gain ammo through any means. The bonus item is lost after being used for the first time, or if the vehicle is Wrecked, or when the game ends.

GAME END

The game ends when one player has more than half the initial crates in their possession, or after the third round, whichever occurs sooner.

VICTORY CONDITIONS

The player holding the most crates at the end of the game is the winner, including any on vehicles that have Scarpered.

SPOILS

If you are playing a Televised Season (see page 156), each team gains D6+1 Cans for each crate held by one of their vehicles at the end of the game. To a maximum of 20 Cans.

THE REVOLUTION WILL BE TELEVISED

While much of the population is content to dream of riches, and the escape afforded by winning a TV game show; an undercurrent of rebellion collects in bars and back rooms across the globe.

The Pro-Earth Resistance seeks to loosen Mars' stranglehold on the Earth and see Earth take its destiny back into her own hands. They are scattered, weak and poorly organised, but always seem to find a way to broadcast their message of freedom and resistance to the sleeping masses.

SETUP

Lay out some terrain to represent a post-apocalyptic wasteland. Each player notes a piece of terrain.

POLE POSITION

Roll-off for Pole Position. At the end of each Gear Phase, pass Pole Position clockwise.

DEPLOYMENT

Each player places a spawn point, which is a round counter no larger than a penny (20mm), on the table within Medium range of any table edge and more than Double range from any other spawn point. Starting with the player with Pole Position, players take it in turns to deploy all of their vehicles within Short range of their spawn point (measured in the same way as a shooting attack). When using Audience Votes to respawn, a vehicle must respawn within Short range of its controller's spawn point.

SPECIAL RULES

- **The Uplink**: At the start of the game, and whenever a new uplink is revealed, the player with Pole Position reveals their noted terrain piece. This terrain piece becomes the uplink, and the players select a new terrain piece. Once per Gear Phase, if a vehicle collides with the uplink, the player controlling the vehicle gains 1 Victory Point, and a new uplink is revealed.
- **Resistance Broadcast**: If you are playing a Televised Season, (see page 156), when a player would gain a Victory Point, they may choose to gain a Resistance Point instead.

GAME END

The game ends when one player has 3 Victory Points, or after three rounds, whichever occurs sooner.

VICTORY CONDITIONS

- **Propaganda:** The player with the most Victory Points at the end of the game is the winner.
- **Censorship**: If you are playing a Televised Season, any player that gained any number of Resistance Points during this game does not gain any Championship Points as a result of this game.

ZOMBIE BASH

The wastelands of the Irradiated States of America are no longer quiet. The graves of a million Americans lie empty, their eerie and radioactive occupants roaming the highways in undead hordes.

SETUP

You will need a large number of roughly 15mm or 20mm zombies or figures to represent the zombies. There should be more than 10 zombies per player.

Lay out some terrain to represent a post-apocalyptic wasteland and arrange the zombies roughly evenly around the play area.

POLE POSITION

Roll-off for Pole Position. At the end of each Gear Phase, pass the Pole Position marker clockwise.

DEPLOYMENT

Starting with the player with Pole Position, players take it in turns to place a spawn point, which is a round counter no larger than a penny (20mm), on the table within Medium range of any table edge and more than Double range from any other spawn point. Then, starting with the player with Pole Position, players take it in turns to deploy all of their vehicles within Short range of their spawn point (measured like a shooting attack). When using Audience Votes to respawn, a vehicle must respawn within Short range of its controller's spawn point.

SPECIAL RULES

- **Zombies:** Vehicles may not attack zombies. Zombies do not count as obstructions. If a vehicle's movement template or Final Position touches a zombie, the controller of that vehicle may collect that zombie. If any vehicle is Wrecked, its controller must place 5 zombies from their collected zombies within Short range of the Wrecked vehicle.
- **Scarper:** Disqualified vehicles do not count as destroyed and may not respawn.

GAME END

The game ends when either fewer than 10 zombies remain in play, or one player has collected 20 zombies, or only one player has vehicles in play, or three rounds have elapsed.

VICTORY CONDITIONS

When the game ends, the player who has collected the most zombies is the winner.

SPOILS

If you are playing a Televised Season (see page 156), each team gains 1 Can for each zombie held at the end of the game, to a maximum of 20 Cans.

SPECIAL EVENTS

BIG GAME HUNTER

"Horrors from the poisoned wastes! Man versus beast, trapped in a deadly struggle! Wheel versus claw! Gas versus guts! Which of our gladiators have the ferocity needed to escape alive?! Vote now for a chance to win a one-in-a-lifetime hunting trip to the Rad Fields of New-New Mexico!"

SETUP

Lay out some terrain to represent a dystopian demolition derby arena.

This scenario requires a select of giant mutated radioactive insects and lizards. You might consider using plastic dinosaurs or oversized insect toys.

POLE POSITION

Players roll-off for Pole Position. At the end of each Gear Phase, pass the Pole Position marker clockwise.

DEPLOYMENT

Players take it in turns to place one giant radioactive creature within Double range of the centre of the table. Then the player with Pole Position deploys one more creature in the centre of the table.

Starting with the player with Pole Position, players then take it in turns to place a spawn point, which is a round counter no larger than a penny (20mm), on the table within Medium range of any table edge and more than Double range from any other spawn point or creature. Then, starting with the player with Pole Position, players take it in turns to deploy all of their vehicles within Short range

of their spawn point (measured like a shooting attack). When using Audience Votes to respawn, a vehicle must respawn within Short range of its controller's spawn point.

GIANT RADIOACTIVE CREATURES

Each giant radioactive Creature is a Heavyweight vehicle with a Crew Value 1 and 20 Hull Points. They cannot roll Skid Dice and do not gain Hazard Tokens. Each creature counts as armed with a Turret mounted Flamethrower with infinite ammo and a Ram on every facing. When attacked, they Evade as if they were in Gear 3. They always declare a Smash Attack reaction. When activated, each creature counts as being in the same current Gear as the current Gear Phase. Each creature may be activated multiple times in a single Gear Phase.

- **Enraged:** Immediately after a vehicle activation in which a creature was targeted with an attack, which caused 2 or more damage to it, the creature activates. The creature is activated by the player that triggered the creature to activate. If multiple creatures are triggered to activate in one activation, the player chooses one creature to activate and the other creatures are not activated.

- **Roar:** At the start of its activation, the creature may choose to make a free pivot. If it does, it must be pivoted to face the last vehicle to attack it.
- **Acidic Ichor**: Once per step, when this creature loses one or more Hull Points, make a 1D6 attack against each vehicle within Medium range at end of that step.

VICTORY CONDITIONS

If a vehicle wrecks a creature, that vehicle's controller gains 1 kill and 2 Audience Votes.

The first team to have 2 creatures (or all the remaining creatures) within Short range of their spawn point is the winner and the game ends. If they are no creatures remaining the game ends, and the team that has most kills is the winner.

DESERT STRIKE

"To celebrate the 20-year anniversary of the heroic Battle of London, in which six hundred brave and patriotic Free Mars pilots defended the inalienable right of Martian independence by firebombing more than twenty square miles of enemy enclaves in the centre of the city of London, we present a unique and deadly game!"

TEAMS

Do not select teams normally. Instead, each player must build a team comprising of only Helicopters and Gyrocopters.

Use of Sponsors is discouraged for this scenario, but if you want to use Sponsors, just say all Sponsors are permitted to purchase Helicopters. As Helicopters are expensive, try this scenario at 70 Cans.

SETUP

Lay out some terrain to represent a dystopian demolition derby arena.

DEPLOYMENT

Deploy 6 rocket turrets in a rough circle, with each turret exactly Double range from the centre of the table.

Starting with the player with Pole Position, players take it in turns to deploy a flag anywhere within Double range of the centre of the table, until there are at least 6 flags in play and every player has deployed at least one flag.

Starting with the player with Pole Position, players take it in turns to deploy one toxic clouds template, which should be roughly the size of a Large Burst template (but the specific size isn't important), until there are at least 6 toxic clouds in play and every player has deployed at least one.

Each player places a spawn point, which is a round counter no larger than a penny (20mm), on the table within Medium range of any table edge and more than Double range from any other spawn point or flag. Starting with the player with Pole Position, players take it in turns to deploy all of their vehicles within Short range of their spawn point (measured like a shooting attack). When using Audience Votes to respawn, a vehicle must respawn within Short range of its controller's spawn point.

SPECIAL RULES

- **Rocket Turrets:** Rocket Turrets count as Middleweight Destructible obstacles with 7 Hull Points. They may be targeted with shooting attacks. If a dropped weapon template overlaps a rocket turret, it will immediately affect them. They always Explode when Wrecked.
- **Camouflaged:** Rocket turrets may only be targeted with shooting attack if the attacking vehicle is within Medium range of the target turret. When Evading, rocket turrets counts as being in Gear 6.
- **Fireworks Show:** If a player wrecks a rocket turret, that player gains 2 Audience Votes.
- **Auto-defense:** At the start of each vehicle's Wipeout Step, each rocket turret will automatically make a 6D6 shooting attack targeting the active vehicle if they are within Long range of the active vehicle. The target may Evade as normal.
- **Toxic Clouds:** These toxic clouds template represent noxious clouds of radioactive dust. These templates cannot be ignored by the Airborne special rule. If a shooting template overlaps a toxic cloud template **before** it touches the target, the target cannot be attacked. Whilst a vehicle is in contact with this dropped weapon template, that vehicle counts as Distracted. If any part of a vehicle's movement template or Final Position touches this dropped weapon template, the vehicle gains 2 Hazard Tokens at the end of its Movement Step.

FLAGS

Flags are Lightweight Destructible obstacles. To represent a flag on the tabletop use an object or miniature approximately 30mm in diameter or smaller. You might use a crate, token, bottle cap, or a literal little flag.

A vehicle may pick up a flag if its movement template or Final Position touches the flag. When picked up, place the flag on the vehicle's dashboard. When a vehicle is Wrecked, the vehicle's owner must place the flag in play, touching the wreck.

At the end of a vehicle's activation, it may place any flag it is carrying within Short range of itself.

GAME END AND VICTORY

The first player to have 2 flags within Short range of their spawn point (either carried or not) is the winner and the game ends. Otherwise, the game ends after three rounds and the player with the most flags either within Short range of their spawn point or carried by a friendly vehicle is the winner.

MONSTER TRUCK SMASH

"And tonight's random draw is… (drum roll please)… Ms Annie McGarnacle! Come on down, Annie! Belt on up! Now's your chance in the driver's seat to win some BIG CASH PRIZES!!!"

SETUP

Lay out some terrain to represent a dystopian demolition derby arena.

TEAM

Players roll off to see who will be the Monster. The other players become the Mice. The Monster player must build a team which may only contain Monster Trucks. The Mice players may build teams as normal.

POLE POSITION

The Monster always has Pole Position during this scenario.

DEPLOYMENT

Each Mice player places a spawn point, which is a round counter no larger than a penny (20mm), on the table within Medium range of any table edge and more than Double range from any other spawn point. The Monster deploys their spawn point in the centre of the table.

Starting with the player with Pole Position, players take it in turns to deploy all of their vehicles within Short range of their spawn point (measured like a shooting attack).

When respawning, a vehicle must respawn within Short range of its controller's spawn point.

After all vehicles are deployed, the Monster deploys 8 flags on the eight points of a compass, with each flag exactly Long range from centre of the table, and not touching terrain.

FLAGS

Flags are Lightweight Destructible obstacles. To represent a flag on the tabletop use an object or miniature approximately 30mm in diameter or smaller. You might use a crate, token, bottle cap, or a literal little flag.

A vehicle may pick up a flag if its movement template or Final Position touches the flag. When picked up, place the flag on the vehicle's dashboard. When a vehicle is Wrecked, vehicle must place any carried flags in play, in contact with the vehicle. If a vehicle carrying a flag is touching another vehicle, it may pass the flag to that vehicle at the end of its activation.

The Monster's vehicles ignore flags at all times.

SPECIAL RULES

- **Squashed**: If one of the Monster's vehicles causes at least one damage to a Mouse controlled vehicle using a Smash Attack, the target vehicle is immediately Wrecked. After being Wrecked, the target's wreck is removed and the Monster player gains 1 Victory Point.
- **Chalk One Up**: If the movement template or Final Position of a vehicle carrying any flags comes within Short range of that team's spawn point, discard all flags and that team scores 2 Victory Points for each flag discarded. Then, that player deploys a new flag exactly Long range from the centre of the table, in one of the empty compass points, not touching terrain or any vehicle.
- **Commercial Break**: At the start of each round, any vehicle that is out of play may be respawned for free within Short range of their spawn point.

GAME END AND VICTORY

If any player has 5 or more Victory Points at the end of any Gear Phase, the games ends. Otherwise, the game ends at the end of the third round. The player with the most Victory Points at the end of the game is the winner.

TANK COMMANDER

"You asked for bigger guns! You asked for bigger explosions! We are but servants. The rest of the week, on pay-to-view, we are bringing you a unique entertainment event, with our guest host: none other than Mr Grant Rutherford himself!"

"Thanks Chip, great to be here. Oh boy, have we got some carnage in store for the folks back home."

TEAMS

Do not select teams normally. Instead, each player is given a Rutherford-sponsored team containing two Tanks only. Each tank is armed with a 125mm Cannon, which begins the game front-mounted.

Use of Sponsors is discouraged for this scenario, but if you want to use Sponsors, just say all Sponsors are permitted to purchase Tanks. You might agree that each player also gains 10 Cans to spend on additional weapons, upgrades and perks.

SETUP

Lay out some terrain to represent a dystopian demolition derby arena.

DEPLOYMENT

Each player places a spawn point, which is a round counter no larger than a penny (20mm), on the table within Medium range of any table edge and more than Double range from any other spawn point. Starting with the player with Pole Position, players take it in turns to deploy all of their vehicles within Short range of their spawn point (measured like a shooting attack). When respawning, a vehicle must respawn within Short range of its controller's spawn point.

SPECIAL RULES

- **Give Them A Good Show**: Tanks have unlimited ammo tokens for their 125mm Cannon. This has the desirable side effect of guaranteeing that all Wrecked Tanks Explode automatically.
- **Audience Participation**: Players may spend 1 Audience Vote to change the facing of their 125mm Cannon to be one of front-mounted, left-mounted, right-mounted, or rear-mounted.
- **On My Mark**: Players may spend 1 Audience Vote to fire an extra shot with their 125mm at any point when they would be allowed to spend Audience Votes. This doesn't count as their attack with that weapon for the purposes of their Attack Step.
- **Close Range**: When any vehicle makes a shooting attack, if the target is within Medium range, the attacking vehicle may re-roll all attack dice that fail to hit.
- **BOOM!**: If a vehicle wrecks an enemy vehicle with a shooting attack, the attacking vehicle's controller gains 2 Audience Votes.
- **Commercial Break**: At the start of each round, any vehicle that is out of play may be respawned for free within Short range of their spawn point.

VICTORY CONDITIONS

If a player successfully causes an enemy tank to become Wrecked, that player gains 1 kill.

The first player to 3 kills is the winner and the game ends.

Feel free to play to 5 Kills for a longer game,
or 2 kills if you have a lot of players.

TRUCKASAURUS

"Legend tells of a beast with skin like steel, whose claws can cut through cars like paper, and whose very breath is white-hot death. From the depths of your nightmares arises a terror so thrilling that you will be unable to resist! For premium subscribers only: Truckasaurus Lives! Screeching out of your television set this Saturday night: 7pm Central Mars Time."

SETUP

Lay out some terrain to represent a dystopian demolition derby arena.

POLE POSITION

Players roll-off for Pole Position. At the end of each Gear Phase, pass the Pole Position marker clockwise.

DEPLOYMENT

Place the Truckasaurus in the centre of the table. The player with Pole Position selects its facing.

Starting with the player with Pole Position, players take it in turns to place a spawn point, which is a round counter no larger than a penny (20mm), on the table within Medium range of any table edge and more than Double range from any other spawn point. Then, starting with the player with Pole Position, players take it in turns to deploy all of their vehicles within Short range of their spawn point (measured in the same way as a shooting attack). When using Audience Votes to respawn, a vehicle must respawn within Short range of its controller's spawn point.

TRUCKASAURUS

Truckasaurus is a Heavyweight vehicle with Handling Value of 2, Crew Value of 4 and infinite Hull Points. It cannot Push It and cannot gain Hazard Tokens. It has the Pivot special rule, and may pivot in any Gear. It has the Up and Over special rule, (see the Monster Truck, page 71). Truckasaurus is armed with a turret-mounted Flamethrower, a turret-mounted 125mm Cannon, a turret-mounted Harpoon, and a Wrecking Ball. It is also equipped with a Ram on every facing and has the Murder Tractor and Boarding Party perks. Truckasaurus is immune to effects caused by weapons. Truckasaurus has infinite ammo for all its weapons.

- **Witness:** If a vehicle declares a Smash Attack against the Truckasaurus during its own activation, that vehicle gains 1 Audience Vote.
- **Truckasaurus Lives:** A player with an active vehicle in play may spend 3 Audience Votes, whenever they would ordinarily be able to spend Audience Votes, to activate the Truckasaurus. When it activates, the

Truckasaurus counts as being in the same current Gear as the current Gear Phase. This activation occurs before the active players activation (if they were about to activate a vehicle). The Truckasaurus may be activated multiple times in a single Gear Phase.

- **Truckasaurus Feeds:** Every time a vehicle is destroyed during Truckasaurus' activation, the player who activated Truckasaurus gains 1 Victory Point. A player may gain a maximum of 1 Victory Point for destroying friendly vehicles during a single Truckasaurus activation.
- **Into the Danger Zone**: If a vehicle begins its activation further than Double range from the Truckasaurus, that vehicle's controller loses 1 Audience Vote.

VICTORY CONDITIONS

The first team to score 5 Victory Points (or 3 Victory Points if there are only two players) is the winner and the game ends. Otherwise, the game ends after three rounds and the player(s) with the most Victory Points is the winner.

CAMPAIGNS

While *Gaslands* can be used to play one-off wasteland scraps or death sports, many players will find it a satisfying experience to play a series of games as a campaign.

Gaslands provides three ways to play a series of linked games. The first is a simple method to grow and expand your teams over time. The second is a simple method to adjudicate a winner after multiple games. The third is for games looking for a more detailed and involved campaign system.

ESCALATING SEASONS

If you want to grow and improve your team over many games, play an Escalating Season.

In an Escalating Season, each team starts with an agreed number of Cans, (30 Cans is recommended). Before each game after the first, each team receives an agreed number of bonus Cans, (10 Cans is recommended), to spend as they please on their team to buy weapons, upgrades, perks and new vehicles. In this way, players will have roughly evenly-matched veteran teams by the end of the season.

If a player joins partway through the season, simply give that player a starting number of Cans equal to the number everyone else has spent so far in this season. For example, if you are playing a season in which player begin with 30 Cans to spend and add 10 Cans before the start of every game after the first, and a player wishes to join just before the fourth game, give that player (30 + 10 + 10 + 10) 60 Cans to build their team and let them get stuck in.

As an alternative, you can also play such you are only permitted to spend your bonus Cans on buy perks and weapons, not new vehicles. This way you start out with basic vehicles and unskilled drivers and get more tooled-up and more awesome during the season, without changing the shape of the team.

CHAMPIONSHIP SEASONS

If you want to adjudicate a final victor at the conclusion of your season, play a Championship Season. It is entirely possible (and recommended) to play an escalating Championship Season.

In a Championship Season, players are awarded Championship Points at the end of each game, according to the position the player came in the game:

CHAMPIONSHIP SEASON TABLE	
Position	Championship Points
1st	5
2nd	3
3rd	1
4th and below	0

TELEVISED SEASONS

If you are looking for a more detailed campaign system for *Gaslands*, the Televised Season rules will allow you to play out a whole *Gaslands* televised racing season, punctuated with wasteland skirmishes to secure the resources needed to fund the next race. Playing a *Gaslands* Televised Season requires two or more players who want to play a series of linked games with the same vehicles, growing and progressing their teams.

SEASON STRUCTURE

A Televised Season consists of a Televised Schedule, containing a fixed number of Televised Events, and any number of Wasteland Skirmishes.

The Televised Events form the "tent-pole" games that provide the overall structure for the campaign and determine its length. These televised events are also the games in which the teams can earn Championship Points, due to the fame and exposure that such events generate.

Outside of these Televised Events, players are free to play as many Wasteland Skirmishes as they like. These Wasteland Skirmishes allow the players to squabble over resources, build up the power of their teams, and prepare for the next Televised Event.

TELEVISED SCHEDULE

To create your season's Televised Schedule, agree how many Televised Events you want to play before announcing a winner then generate the scenario that each event will be. Establish this Televised Schedule prior to the first game in the season.

For each Televised Event in your schedule, generate a scenario using this table (or choose):

TELEVISED EVENT SCHEDULE TABLE	
D6	Scenario
1–2	Death Race
3	Arena of Death
4	Capture the Flag
5	Flag Tag
6	Saturday Night Live

WASTELAND SKIRMISHES

When you meet up, as long as more than half of the players in your race season are present, play the next Televised Event in the Televised Schedule. Otherwise, or if all players prefer, play a Wasteland Skirmish scenario. You can generate a scenario using this table (or choose):

WASTELAND SKIRMISH TABLE	
D6	**Scenario**
1	Automated Salvage
2	Express Delivery
3–4	Scavenger Party
5	The Revolution Will Be Televised
6	Zombie Bash

PRO-EARTH RESISTANCE

Teams may gain Resistance Points during the season, particularly if they are doing badly in the race season. They are mostly kept secret.

Before any Televised Event game, if the last game was not "The Revolution Will Be Televised", a player that has not yet triggered "The Revolution Will Be Televised" scenario, may reveal a number Resistance Points that exceeds the total number of players that started the campaign to force the next game to use "The Revolution Will Be Televised" scenario. "The Revolution Will Be Televised" replaces the scheduled Televised Event.

WINNING THE SEASON

After the final Televised Event in the season, the team with the most Championship Points is awarded the title of *Gaslands* Season Champion.

If there is a tie for the most Championship Points, award the title of *Gaslands* Season Champion to the player with the fewest Resistance Points.

In addition, if at least one game of "The Revolution Will Be Televised" was played, then the team with the most Resistance Points at the end of the season is awarded the title of Pro-Earth Resistance General.

HIRE TEAMS

At the start of the season, players receive 30 Cans to purchase their initial teams. Each player selects a Sponsor and then purchases vehicles, weapons, upgrades, and perks.

Once hired, this team cannot be altered from game to other, other than using the Scrapping Vehicles and Spending Spoils rules (see page 164). This is now the player's team for the duration of the race season. If you wish to start with fewer or more Cans, starting team sizes of anywhere between 20 and 50 Cans work's great.

Team may never contain more than 8 vehicles at any point during the season.

PRE-GAME SEQUENCE
HANDICAP BONUS

Before each game, compare the Championship Points of each team with the Championship Points of the team with the most Championship Points. Teams with fewer Championship Points may gain bonus Audience Votes at the start of the game, to use during that game:

HANDICAP BONUS TABLE	
Difference in Championship Points	Bonus Audience Votes
0–10	-
11–15	1 Audience Vote
16–20	2 Audience Votes
21–25	3 Audience Votes
26–30	4 Audience Votes
31+	5 Audience Votes

All unspent Audience Votes are lost between games.

SABOTAGE TOKENS

Before each Televised Event, a player with 3 or more Resistance Points may secretly take one Sabotage Token per 3 Resistance Points they have.

During the game, the player may reveal the number of Resistance Points they have and spend a Sabotage Token to trigger any of the following effects:

- **Hidden Explosives**: At any point, this player may spend a Sabotage Token to select a point anywhere on the table. This point explodes: immediately make a 4D6 attack with the Blast special rule against every vehicle within Medium range.
- **Do Not Adjust Your Set**: When a player would normally be able to spend Audience Votes, this player may spend a Sabotage Token to activate any single Audience Vote effect.
- **Fix Your Brakes**: Immediately before a Flip check, this player may spend a Sabotage Token to cause the vehicle to automatically Flip without rolling.
- **Resistance Cache**: At the start of a vehicle's activation, this player may spend a Sabotage Token to immediately give the active vehicle a Grenades weapon with 5 ammo tokens.

After revealing their Resistance Points and spending their first sabotage token of the game, the player may not gain or spend Audience Votes for the remainder of the game.

POST-GAME SEQUENCE

After each campaign game, you go through the following steps:

- Spoils
- Contacting the Resistance
- Damage and Injuries
- Workshop

SPOILS

The goal of the season is to progress to the big leagues and ultimately to Mars, and the actions and heroics of the team drivers contribute to the teams overall fame and reputation, helping to secure them advertising and sponsorship deals.

To represent this, actions and achievements during a game reward the team. Doing well in televised events can also award the team Championship Points, which are what is needed to win the season. Doing well in wastelands skirmishing can provide the money needed to repair and improve the team.

After the game, check the following table, and add any Cans to the team's stash and any Championship Points to the team's Championship Points total:

SPOILS TABLE		
Events	Cans	Championship Points
1st place in a Televised Event game.		+10
2nd place in a Televised Event game.		+5
3rd place in a Televised Event game.		+2
4th place in a Televised Event game.		+1
Each gate passed by at least one of this team's vehicle in a Death Race.		+1
Team took part in a Wasteland Skirmish game.	D6	-
For each enemy Lightweight vehicle Wrecked by this team.	-	+1
For each enemy Middleweight vehicle Wrecked by this team.	-	+2
For each enemy Heavyweight vehicle Wrecked by this team.	-	+3
For each enemy War Rig Wrecked by this team.	-	+5
Player fielded a team of fully-painted models for the first time (once per player, per campaign, after game).	-	+5
Player fielded a custom converted model for the first time (once per player, per campaign, after game).	-	+5

Teams can only gain Championship Points if the game was part of the Televised Schedule.

When awarding "places", only half (rounding up) of the competing players may place. The rest gain no Championship Points.

STASH

Any Cans that you haven't spent yet go in your Stash.

CONTACTING THE RESISTANCE

If a team did not "place" during this game, that team may secretly choose to contact the Pro-Earth Resistance in order to gain 3 Resistance Points. This fact must be written down secretly.

DAMAGE AND INJURIES

Any vehicle that was Wrecked during the game must roll a D6, and add the number of dents that it has, to see what happens to it. If the vehicle is lightweight, add 1 to the roll. If the vehicle is heavyweight, subtract 1 from the roll.

VEHICLE WRECKED TABLE	
D6 + Dents	**Result**
0–1	Popped it back in! -1 Dent (to a minimum of 0).
2–3	Escaped unscathed: no effect.
4	Bent wheel-arch: +1 Dent.
5	Blown off: Permanently lose a randomly-selected weapon or upgrade. +1 Dent.
6	Wrecked pinion: Permanently lose a randomly-selected perk. +1 Dent.
7	Upholstery ruined: Permanently reduce Crew Value by 1 (to a minimum of 1). +2 Dents.
8	Weakened chassis: +1 Hazard Token when involved in a Collision. +2 Dents.
9	Audience Favourite: If this vehicle is Wrecked, its controller immediately discards 3 Audience Votes (to a minimum of 0). +5 Championship Points. +3 Dents.
10+	Vehicle destroyed, Driver Dead.

Lost perks and weapons may be re-bought using Cans from your stash.

VEHICLE DESTROYED, DRIVER DEAD

When a vehicle suffers the "Vehicle Destroyed, Driver Dead" result, you must permanently remove that vehicle from your team. All weapons, upgrades and perks on that vehicle are also permanently lost.

DENTS

Most of the results on the Vehicle Wrecked table give the vehicle a number of Dents. Record the number of dents each vehicle has received on that vehicle's dashboard. They have no effect during the game, but affect the "vehicle Wrecked" roll above, and may be spent on Injuries.

INJURIES

Dents may be exchanged to purchase from a set of special perks, called Injuries. This may be done before or after a game and before or after the roll on the Vehicle Wrecked table (see page 162). These perks aren't all positive but spending Dents on Injuries will keep your vehicle in play for longer.

A vehicle may have any number of Injuries, but may not have the same Injury twice. After selecting an Injury, remove the listed number of Dents from the vehicle.

- **Deathwish (-1 Dent)**: This vehicle cannot choose to Shift down.
- **Bad Television (-1 Dent):** This vehicle must pay one additional Audience Vote to respawn.
- **Crazed (-2 Dents)**: This vehicle may not use Shift results to cancel out Spin or Slide results.
- **Cowardly (-2 Dents)**: This vehicle must always declare an Evade during a Collision, they may not declare a Smash Attack.
- **Old War Wound (-3 Dents)**: At the start of every game, roll a D6. On a 1, this vehicle cannot take part in this game.
- **Shakes (-3 Dents)**: This vehicle wipes out at 5 Hazard Tokens instead of 6.
- **Twitch (-4 Dents)**: At the start of the game, you must inform your opponents which of your drivers have the Twitch Injury. Once per game, when this driver is about to roll their Skid Dice, any opponent may declare: "Twitch". That opponent may roll the Skid Dice, instead of you, and choose how to resolve them. The twitching vehicle may not Push It. A driver may only be affected by Twitch once per game.
- **Held Together by Rust (-5 Dents)**: During the Post-Game Sequence, when rolling on the Vehicle Wrecked table (see page 162), apply the first result then roll again and apply the second result as well.
- **Badass (-6 Dents)**: This vehicle may immediately select and gain any one Badass perk, without paying its cost, even if this driver could not normally select Badass perks.
- **Living Legend (-11 Dents)**: During the Post-Game Sequence, when rolling on the Vehicle Wrecked table (see page 162), count your result as 1 and remove any injury perks you wish.

SCRAPPING VEHICLES

You may sell vehicles, weapons, or upgrades that you don't want for half their cost, rounding down. You get nothing for selling perks.

SPENDING SPOILS

Your Cans of gasoline may be traded in to buy stuff for your team:

- Buy new vehicles.
- Buy new weapons or upgrades.
- Buy vehicle a new perk.

The spoils of a game may be spent on any member of the team and may also be stashed away for a larger purchase in the future.

You can buy anything from the lists of the vehicles, weapons, upgrades, and perks, as long as your team would normally access to buy that item during team construction.

MOVING PERKS AROUND

In GASLANDS, crew and perks are permanently associated with their vehicle. A perk may not be transferred from one vehicle to another. When you sell a vehicle, you lose all its perks. When you buy a new vehicle, that vehicle has no perks.

SAVAGE HIGHWAYS

A team's War Rig is their fortress. It is a mobile garage, workshop, storeroom, production studio, armoury, rec room, green room, and home. It is decorated with the team's logos and sponsors and contains pretty much everything they hold dear in this ruined world.

Teams must travel great distances to get from one big event to the next. The journeys are long and treacherous, and the teams' itineraries are unfortunately a matter for public broadcast. Gangs of thieves, raiders, highwaymen, and pirates lie in wait for these juicy targets, and a team must be ready to outrun or outgun these bandits if they want to survive long enough to make it to the big leagues.

There have been endless requests to the *Gaslands* producers for better protection for teams in transit, but the response is always that resources are stretched too thin. Oddly enough, there always seem to be enough resources to get a helicopter with a camera crew airborne when the raiders strike.

NARRATIVE CAMPAIGN

Savage Highways is a campaign of three narratively-linked games of *Gaslands*, for two or more players. One player is chosen to represent the **Riggers**, and the remaining players become the **Gangers**. This campaign can be played standalone, or as a bridge between two televised events.

Unlike regular *Gaslands* scenarios, which don't require any specific table size, *Savage Highways* is designed to be played on an approximately 4' x 4' table.

The campaign always begins with **Scenario 1: Escape The City**.

© Jeffrey Kelly

RIGGERS

The **Riggers** receive a War Rig, and 20 Cans with which to add weapons and upgrades to it. The War Rig may not be given any perks and may not be given a Nitro Booster or any electrical upgrades.

The Riggers then receive 60 more Cans with which to purchase the rest of their team, including further weapons and upgrades for their War Rig. They may not purchase a second War Rig.

GANGERS

The **Gangers** players receive 120 Cans in total, split equally among the players, to purchase teams of their own. Each player is free to select a Sponsor individually. Gangers may not purchase War Rigs.

If you are playing with multiple Ganger players, be sure to use the Team Games rules on page 123.

WAR RIG UPGRADES

During the campaign, the Riggers' War Rig can receive and lose five possible War Rig Upgrades. The Riggers' War Rig may have any number of these upgrades at any time. These upgrades require no build slots. The Riggers' War Rig may not have more than one of each named upgrade at any time. Only one upgrade may be removed during an activation by any means.

- **Hangers On**: this vehicle increases its Crew Value by 4. If this vehicle is involved in two or more Collisions in a single activation, discard this upgrade as the crew are flung wildly from the vehicle.
- **Selvaggio**: Once per round, this vehicle may remove 1 Hull Point in order to discard all Hazard Tokens. If this vehicle is targeted by two shooting attacks in a single Gear Phase that do not suffer from cover in a single Gear Phase, discard this upgrade as the snipers find their mark.
- **Fuel Pod**: Once per Gear Phase, this vehicle may discard or re-roll one Skid Die. If an enemy vehicle ever declares a tailgate Smash Attack that rolls no attack dice, discard this upgrade as the raiders cut the fuel lines and siphon them off.
- **Grease Monkey**: Once per Gear Phase, if this vehicle successfully evades a hit during an attack, gain 1 previously lost Hull Point. If this vehicle ever gains a Hazard Token via the Blast special rule, discard this upgrade as the mechanic is thrown from the rig.
- **Cow Catcher**: Once per round, this vehicle may consider a single piece of terrain to be Destructible during its activation. If this vehicle is involved with a Head-on Collision with a Ganger vehicle, discard this upgrade.

SPECIAL RULES

These rules apply throughout the campaign.

- **Ride Eternal:** After each game, Wrecked vehicles are regained prior to the next game, have their Hull Value permanently reduced by 2, meaning that they will start the next game with 2 fewer Hull Points.
- **Unlikely Stamina:** The War Rig cannot be Wrecked if it has any War Rig Upgrades attached, even if has lost all its Hull Points. When the War Rig has lost all its Hull Points and has no War Rig Upgrades attached then it is immediately Wrecked.
- **Plot Immunity:** The Riggers' War Rig cannot be affected by the Death Ray weapon.

SCENARIO 1: ESCAPE THE CITY

"Our troubles started before we even hit the city limits. Ramshackle as the jury-rigged barricades looked, the wild eyes of the wasters gave us pause. No matter: there was no way on hell we were slowing down for these clowns."

SETUP

Lay out some terrain to represent a post-apocalyptic wasteland.

DEPLOYMENT

The **Riggers** must select and attach a single War Rig Upgrade to their War Rig. The Riggers deploy their War Rig touching any table edge, which becomes the Riggers' table edge. They then deploy the rest of their vehicles touching the Riggers' table edge.

The **Gangers** deploy their teams in any order the Gangers agree. Gangers deploy on the table edge opposite the Riggers' table edge, which becomes the Gangers' table edge. in any order the Gangers agree. Each Ganger player deploys their first vehicle touching any point on the Gangers' table edge, and then places their remaining vehicles within Medium range of the first vehicle, touching the Gangers' table edge.

- **Respawn:** When using Audience Votes to respawn, a vehicle must respawn in contact with their table edge.
- **Road Blocks**: After all vehicles are deployed, the Gangers may deploy two pieces of scenery, each no longer than Medium range and no wider than Short range, anywhere completely outside of Long range of the War Rig.

POLE POSITION

A Gangers player selected by the Gangers starts the game with Pole Position. At the end of each Gear Phase, Pole Position swaps from the Gangers to the Riggers or vice versa.

VICTORY CONDITIONS

- If the Riggers' War Rig touches the Gangers' table edge, it escapes and the game ends. The game also ends if the Riggers' War Rig is disqualified or is Wrecked.
- If the Riggers' War Rig escapes, the Riggers win, otherwise, the Gangers win.

© James Hall

If the Gangers win, the War Rig Upgrade selected during setup is permanently lost and cannot be selected again during this campaign. Play **Scenario 2A: Rescue** next (see page 169).

If the Riggers win, the War Rig Upgrade selected during setup is automatically re-attached to the War Rig at the start of every following scenario in this campaign. Play **Scenario 2B: Ambush** next (see page 172)

SCENARIO 2A: RESCUE

"The raiders loaded up what they could carry and posted a guard while they tore off to stash the first of the loot. As the storm came in, this was our chance to use the confusion to recover our precious rig."

SETUP

Lay out some terrain to represent a post-apocalyptic wasteland.

The Gangers must select and attach to the Riggers' War Rig a single War Rig Upgrade that has not previously been attached to the Riggers' War Rig in this campaign.

DEPLOYMENT

The **Riggers** first deploy their War Rig in the centre of any table edge. They then deploy the rest of their vehicles touching the table edge opposite the Riggers' War Rig, which becomes the Riggers' table edge.

The **Gangers** deploy their teams in any order they agree, with each Ganger player placing their first vehicle touching any point on either of the table edges that do not have Rigger vehicles on, and then placing their remaining vehicles within medium of the first vehicle, touching the same table edge.

- **Respawn:** When using Audience Votes to respawn, a vehicle must respawn in contact with their table edge.

SPECIAL RULES

- **Sandstorm**: At the end the first turn, the Gangers players may pivot the War Rig up to 90 degrees in either direction (causing a Collision Window), as the War Rig driver loses her bearings in the sandstorm.

POLE POSITION

A Ganger player selected by the Gangers starts the game with Pole Position. At the end of each Gear Phase, Pole Position swaps from the Gangers to the Riggers or vice versa.

GAME END

If the Riggers' War Rig touches the Riggers' board edge, it escapes, and the game ends. The game also ends if a Gear Phase beings with the Rigger's War Rig either disqualified or Wrecked.

VICTORY CONDITIONS

If the Rigger's War Rig escapes, the Riggers win, otherwise, the Gangers win.

If the Gangers win, the War Rig Upgrade selected during setup is permanently lost and cannot be selected again during this campaign. Play **Scenario 3: Long Road Home** next.

If the Riggers win, the War Rig Upgrade selected during setup is automatically re-attached to the War Rig at the start of every following scenario in this campaign. Play **Scenario 3: Long Road Home** next.

SCENARIO 2B: AMBUSH

"The rickety roadblocks couldn't hold us, but the scavengers' pursuit was relentless and hard. As darkness started to fall, we headed into the perilous nano-sumps of the irradiated grey wastes, hoping to shake them."

SETUP

Lay out some terrain to represent a post-apocalyptic wasteland.

The Riggers must select and attach a single War Rig Upgrade to their War Rig.

- **Swamps**: The Riggers may place three pieces of treacherous terrain, no more than Medium range in diameter, anywhere on the table, which represent swamps, quicksand, sinkholes, or ice flows (depending on your scenery theme).

DEPLOYMENT

The **Riggers** deploys their War Rig in the centre of the table, directly facing any table edge. This table edge becomes the Riggers' table edge. The Riggers then deploy the rest of their vehicles touching the Riggers' table edge.

The **Gangers** take turns deploying their teams in any order the Gangers agree. Gangers deploy their first vehicle touching any point on either of the two table edges perpendicular to the Rigger's table edge, which become the Gangers' table edges, and then place their remaining vehicles within Medium range of the first vehicle, touching the same table edge.

- **Respawn:** When using Audience Votes to respawn, a vehicle must respawn in contact with any of their table edges.

SPECIAL RULES

The Riggers' War Rig begins Wrecked, and this wreck cannot be removed from play. If a vehicle controlled by the Rigger's moves within Short range of the War Rig, then the War Rig respawns in place and may be activated as normal from that point on (as someone hops into the cab to start the engine).

POLE POSITION

A Ganger player selected by the Gangers starts the game with Pole Position. At the end of each Gear Phase, Pole Position swaps from the Gangers to the Riggers or vice versa.

GAME END

If the Riggers' War Rig touches either of the Gangers table edges, it escapes and the game ends. The game also ends if a Gear Phase begins with the Rigger's War Rig either disqualified or Wrecked.

VICTORY CONDITIONS

If the Riggers' War Rig touches either of the Gangers table edges, it escapes and the game ends. The game also ends if a Gear Phase begins with the Rigger's War Rig either disqualified or Wrecked.

If the Rigger's War Rig escapes, the Riggers win, otherwise, the Gangers win.

If the Gangers win, the War Rig Upgrade selected during setup is permanently lost and cannot be selected again during this campaign. Play **Scenario 3: Long Road Home** next.

If the Riggers win, the War Rig Upgrade selected during setup is automatically re-attached to the War Rig at the start of every following scenario in this campaign. Play **Scenario 3: Long Road Home** next.

SCENARIO 3: LONG ROAD HOME

"With our destination fast approaching, our pursuers have put in a last-ditch effort to finish us off. A long, broken highway connected us with the relatively safety of the next arena. We just needed to survive long enough to make it to the bright lights of the city."

SETUP

Lay out some sparse terrain to represent a post-apocalyptic wasteland. You might choose to place a long, straight road surface down the middle of the table.

The Riggers must select and attach exactly three War Rig Upgrades to their War Rig, in addition to any upgrades automatically attached due to winning either of the previous scenarios.

The Riggers select a single table edge to be the Entry Edge. The table edge opposite the entry edge becomes the Exit Edge.

DEPLOYMENT

The **Riggers** deploys their War Rig in the centre of the entry edge, and deploys the rest of their vehicles within Medium range of the War Rig.

The **Gangers** take turns deploying their teams in any order the Gangers agree.

Gangers deploy their first vehicle touching any point on the entry edge, and then place their remaining vehicles within Medium range of the first vehicle, touching the entry edge. No Ganger vehicle may be deployed within Double range of the War Rig.

Respawn: When using Audience Votes to respawn, a vehicle must respawn in contact with the entry edge.

POLE POSITION

A Ganger player selected by the Gangers starts the game with Pole Position. At the end of each Gear Phase, Pole Position swaps from the Gangers to the Riggers or vice versa.

ROLLING ROAD

If the War Rig touches the exit edge, the Riggers gain 1 Victory Point, and the War Rig is removed from play. Mark any vehicle that touches the exit edge in the same Gear Phase that the War Rig exits as "1". Mark vehicles exiting the table in the following Gear Phase (even if this is during the following round) as "2" and so on. Mark the place that each vehicle exits the table (perhaps by just leaving the vehicle on the edge of the table with a dice on it to indicate its marked number). All vehicles still in play after the Gear Phase marking vehicles as "6" are disqualified.

When no vehicles are on the table, rearrange the terrain and start a new round. No terrain may be placed within Long range of the entry edge. This counts as a new table.

Deploy all vehicles marked "1" at the start of Gear Phase 1, "2" at the start of Gear Phase 2 and so on. When deploying vehicles, they must be placed touching the entry edge, and exactly in line with the point on the exit edge that they exited the previous table. These vehicles remain in the same Gear that they exited the table in.

SPECIAL RULES

- **Wheeled Army**: The Gangers may respawn vehicles even if they have other vehicles in play. If the Rigger player has 0 Victory Points, Ganger players may respawn vehicles for the cost of 1 Audience Vote. If the Rigger player has 1 Victory Point, Ganger players may respawn vehicles for the cost of 2 Audience Votes. If the Rigger player has 2 Victory Points, Ganger players may not respawn vehicles.
- **Desperate Flight**: The Rigger player may not use the War Rig's Tanker Anchor special rule during this game.

GAME END

The game ends when either the Riggers have scored 3 Victory Points, or a Gear Phase begins with the Rigger's War Rig either disqualified or Wrecked.

VICTORY CONDITIONS

At the end of the game, if the Riggers have scored 3 Victory Points, they win. Otherwise, the Gangers win. **The winner of this scenario is the overall winner of the campaign!**

- **Rigger Victory**: *Machine gun nests light up the remaining gangers, as enthusiastic and underpaid intern gunners seek to prove they have what it takes to make it in television. The War Rig rumbles into the huge arena, sporting an array of glamorous battle scars. The and the crowd erupts with joy.*
- **Ganger Victory**: *The War Rig is a treasure trove of munitions, hardware, spare parts and sweet, heady gasoline. The bones of the rig are picked clean and left, like the carcass of some steel behemoth, to bake in the harsh wasteland sun. With a haul like this, you could make it to the big leagues.*

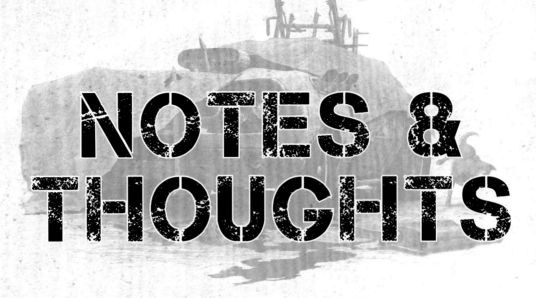

NOTES & THOUGHTS

ORGANISED PLAY

Current rules and guidelines for organised play for *Gaslands* are available at Gaslands.com. We love it when people run events, so make sure to let us know and we'll do what we can to let others know about it.

TEMPLATES AND DICE

You can get hold of high-quality *Gaslands* templates, tokens, Skid Dice and terrain from a host of fantastic Friends of Gaslands Across the world, all discoverable from Gaslands.com/store.

RACETRACK LAYOUTS

The layout you choose for your *Gaslands* Death Race can make a big difference to the length of the game and the amount of interaction between the lead vehicles and the laggards. Visit Gaslands.com to see layouts that other players have submitted, and to submit your own.

GAMES TAKING TOO LONG?

If you find that *Gaslands* is running a little long for you, particularly when playing with more players, try the following recommendations: play with fewer Cans, such as 25 per player, only permit one or two vehicles per player, and ignore the "Touch It, Use It" rule if players are agonising over their template choices. If you are playing the Death Race scenario, place the gates closer together.

RULE UNCLEAR?

If you are struggling to understand a rule in *Gaslands*, be sure to first read the rule carefully and thoroughly. If that does not clear the matter up, read the sections that pertain to the other concepts used in this situation. If the answer is still unclear: apply the Rule of Carnage to keep the game moving, and then take a look at the official FAQ document, which is available to download from the *Gaslands* website.

If none of this solves the issue, feel free to ask in the forums on the *Gaslands* website, on BoardGameGeek, or in the official *Gaslands* Facebook Group. Final tip: just because you saw it played that way at your FLGS or in a YouTube battle report, it doesn't mean that's how the rule works! Trust your reading of the text in this rulebook.

BASES

You are not required to base your vehicles, the choice is yours. Toy cars tend to have a pretty regular footprint, so you shouldn't find too many issues unless your converted vehicles are particularly crazy. If you don't use bases, all measurements are from and to the body of the vehicle.

If you use bases, all measurements are made from and to the bases.

If you do choose to use bases, the minimum recommended sizes are as follows:

GASLANDS BASE SIZE TABLE	
Vehicle	**Minimum Base Size**
Bikes	20mm x 30mm
Most vehicles	30mm x 60mm
Heavyweight vehicles	40mm x 80mm
Bus	40mm x 100mm
War Rig	CAB: 50mm x 80mm TRAILER: 50mm x 150mm

CHANGING THE SCALE

Because everything is managed using the movement template, *Gaslands* scales perfectly to different sizes of model cars. To play *Gaslands* with 28mm scale vehicles, simply photocopy the templates at 130% original size (i.e. from A4 to A3) and use a larger table. To play *Gaslands* with 10mm, 15mm, or "micro" scale vehicles, just photocopy the templates at 70% original size (i.e. from A4 to A5).

CHANGING THE SETTING

The *Gaslands* rules are perfectly suited to a range of settings outside of the post-apocalyptic one we provide.

You might use these rules to play games based on 1970s cop shows, wacky races, pod racing, space-orc buggy battles, Hollywood action chase sequences, NASCAR, Formula One, caveman car racing, powerboat racing, a robotic rally on a factory floor, a breakfast-table micro-machines race, skateboards or hoverboards, skiing, bicycle racing, zero-gravity EVA or jetpack combat, banger racing, demolition derby, motor-X, monster truck shows, and (maybe) even chariot racing.

Gaslands should suit most any kind of vehicle racing situation, or any situation where you need to simulate the competitors having momentum rather than be able to change direction at will.

Find out more at Gaslands.com

CREDITS

PLANET SMASHER GAMES

Gaslands is a Planet Smasher game. Check out more great games at:
PlanetSmasherGames.com

GAME DESIGN

Mike Hutchinson

GAME DEVELOPMENT

Glenn Ford   John Brindley

GASLANDS REFUELLED PLAYTESTING HEROES

Joe Wood   Brian Freitas
Phil Hawtin   Kyle Greiner
Jay Newell   Anthony Amato Jr.
David Brennan   Dominic Parker

PLAYTESTING

Thank you to everyone that took part in the original beta testing prior to the game's release, and to everyone that helped with playtesting this revised and expanded edition. There are too many awesome people to list here, so check them all out at Gaslands.com/playtesters.

PHOTOGRAPHS

Mike Hutchinson, Jake Zettelmaier, James Hall, Jeffrey Kelly and Sven Siewert

ACKNOWLEDGEMENTS

Thank you to John Brindley for the original concept, Glenn Ford for all his generous support both in developing the game and also promoting it, Gav Thorpe for lending me his copy of Dark Future, and to everyone in the incredible *Gaslands* Facebook community (which is my favourite place on the Internet). Thanks to Ramshackle Games, S&S Models, and TTCombat for use of their terrain and conversion bits throughout this book.

QUICK REFERENCE

FULL TIMING STEPS

Each Round proceeds through Gear Phases 1 to 6. In each Gear Phase, activate each vehicle in that Gear or higher, starting with the player in Pole Position and proceeding clockwise.

When a player has an opportunity to activate a vehicle, follow these steps:

- Optionally spend Audience Votes
- Select a qualifying vehicle to activate, or pass
- Activate selected vehicle:
  1. Movement Step
  2. Attack Step
  3. Wipeout Step

MOVEMENT STEP

1.1. **Select** a movement template.

1.2. **Place** the movement template.

1.3. **Roll some Skid Dice**, up to Handling Value of vehicle.

1.4. **Spend Shift results**:
- Discard one hazard, slide or spin result.
- Change Gear up or down by 1, +1 Hazard Token.
- Discard one Hazard Token from this vehicle.
- Discard without effect.

1.5. **Gain Hazard Tokens** from hazard, slide and spin results.

1.6. **Place Slide template**, if the vehicle had an uncancelled slide result.

1.7. **Move** the vehicle into its Final Position.

COLLISION WINDOW

1.8. **Spin** the vehicle, if the vehicle had an uncancelled spins result.

COLLISION WINDOW

ATTACK STEP

2.1 **Declare targets** and check range and cover.

2.3 **Roll Attack Dice**: 4+ to hit, 6 is critical (2 hits).

COLLISION WINDOW

2.4 **Evade**: Each 6+ cancels one hit.

2.5 **Damage**: Remove Hull Points.

WIPEOUT

3.1 **Flip check**: Roll D6, if lower than current Gear then suffer 2 hits and forced move medium straight forward.

COLLISION WINDOW

3.2 **Reset**: Regardless of flip check, reduce current Gear to 1 and discard all Hazard Tokens from the vehicle.

3.3 **Lose Control**: Regardless of flip check, the player clockwise of the player controlling the active vehicle pivots the vehicle about its centre point to any facing.

COLLISION WINDOW

COLLISIONS

1. Determine orientation.
2. Active vehicle declares reaction.
3. Passive vehicle or obstacle declares reaction.
4. Roll any Smash Attacks.
5. Roll any evades.
6. Apply un-cancelled hits .

If both parties evaded, gain 1 Hazard Token each, else both gain 2 Hazard Tokens

COLLISION TABLE	
Orientation	Smash Attack Dice
Head On	Sum of current Gears: Each vehicle uses their current Gear plus the other participant's current Gear.
T-bone	Vehicle's own current Gear.
Tailgate	Difference in current Gears: Each vehicle uses the faster participant's current Gear minus the slower participant's current Gear, to a minimum of zero.

COLLISION DICE TABLE	
Bonus	Bonus Smash Attack Dice
1 Class Heavier	+2 attack dice
2 Classes Heavier	+4 attack dice
1 Class Lighter	-1 attack die
2 Classes Lighter	-2 attack dice

GETTING WRECKED

1   **Skid to A Halt:** Forced move short straight forward
COLLISION WINDOW
2   **Reset:** Reduce current Gear to 1 and discard all Hazard Tokens from the vehicle
3   **Explosion Check:** Roll D6 + ammo tokens, explodes on 6+
4   **Get Wrecked:** Turn model over, leave in play as a wreck

EXPLOSIONS

EXPLOSION TABLE	
Weight	Explosion Attack Dice
Lightweight	2D6
Middleweight	4D6
Heavyweight	6D6

SPENDING AUDIENCE VOTES

- **1 Vote:** BURN RUBBER: Change Gear. THUNDEROUS APPLAUSE: Remove D6 Hazard Tokens from that vehicle.
- **2 Votes:** EXECUTIVE INTERVENTION: Put enemy vehicle on 5 Hazard Tokens. RELOAD: +1 ammo token. CARPE DIEM: Take/give Pole Position, or prevent its next move.
- **3 Votes:** RESPAWN: If you have no vehicles currently in play, respawn one vehicle which suffers damage equal to half its Hull Value, rounded up.

VEHICLES

Vehicle Type	Weight	Hull	Handling	Max Gear	Crew	Build Slots	Special Rules	Cost
Drag Racer	Lightweight	4	4	6	1	2	Jet Engine.	5
Bike	Lightweight	4	5	6	1	1	Full Throttle. Pivot.	5
Buggy	Lightweight	6	4	6	2	2	Roll Cage.	6
Bike with Sidecar	Lightweight	4	5	6	2	2	Full Throttle. Pivot.	8
Ice-cream Truck	Middleweight	10	2	4	2	2	Infuriating Jingle.	8
Car	Middleweight	10	3	5	2	2		12
Performance Car	Middleweight	8	4	6	1	2	Slip Away.	15
Truck	Middleweight	12	2	4	3	3		15
Gyrocopter	Middleweight	4	4	6	1	0	Airwolf. Airborne.	10
Ambulance	Middleweight	12	2	5	3	3	Uppers. Downers.	20
Monster Truck	Heavyweight	10	3	4	2	2	All Terrain. Up and Over.	25
Heavy Truck	Heavyweight	14	2	3	4	5		25
Bus	Heavyweight	16	2	3	8	3		30
Helicopter	Heavyweight	8	3	4	3	4	Airwolf. Airborne. Restricted	30
Tank	Heavyweight	20	4	3	3	4	Pivot. Up and Over. All Terrain. Turret. Restricted	40
War Rig	Heavyweight	26	2	4	5	5	See War Rig rules.	40

WEAPONS

Weapon Name	Range	Attack Dice	Special Rules	Build Slots	Cost
125mm Cannon	Double	8D6	Ammo 3. Blast. See special rules, page 72.	3	6
Arc Lightning Projector	Double	6D6	Ammo 1. Electrical. See special rules, page 73.	2	6**
Bazooka	Double	3D6	Ammo 3. Blast.	2	4
BFG	Double	10D6	Ammo 1. See special rules, page 73.	3	1
Blunderbuss	Small Burst	2D6	Crew Fired. Splash.	-	2
Caltrop Dropper	Dropped	2D6	Ammo 3. Small Burst. See special rules, page 79.	1	1
Combat Laser	Double	3D6	Splash. See special rules.	1	5
Death Ray	Double	3D6	Ammo 1. Electrical. See special rules, page 73.	1	3
Flamethrower	Large Burst	6D6	Ammo 3. Splash. Fire. Indirect.	2	4
Gas Grenades	Medium	(1D6)	Ammo 5. Crew Fired. Indirect. Blitz. See special rules, page 76.	-	1
Glue Dropper	Dropped	-	Ammo 1. See special rules, page 79.	1	1
Grabber Arm	Short	3D6	See special rules.	1	6
Grav Gun	Double	(3D6)	Ammo 1. Electrical. See special rules, page 73.	1	2**
Grenades	Medium	1D6	Ammo 5. Crew Fired. Blast. Indirect. Blitz.	-	1
Handgun	Medium	1D6	Crew Fired.	-	-
Harpoon	Double	(5D6)	See special rules, page 74.	1	2
Heavy Machine Gun	Double	3D6		1	3
Kinetic Super Booster	Double	(6D6)	Ammo 1. Electrical. See special rules, page 74.	2	6**
Machine Gun	Double	2D6		1	2
Magnetic Jammer	Double	-	Electrical. See special rules, page 74.	-	2**
Magnum	Double	1D6	Crew Fired. Blast.	-	3
Mine Dropper	Dropped	4D6	Ammo 3. Small Burst. Blast. See special rules, page 79.	1	1
Minigun	Double	4D6		1	5
Molotov Cocktails	Medium	1D6	Ammo 5. Crew Fired. Fire. Indirect. Blitz.	-	1
Mortar	Double	4D6	Ammo 3. Indirect.	1	4
Napalm Dropper	Dropped	4D6	Ammo 3. Small Burst. Fire. See special rules, page 79.	1	1
Oil Slick Dropper	Dropped	-	Ammo 3. See special rules, page 79.	-	2
RC Car Bombs	Dropped	4D6	Ammo 3. See special rules, page 79.	-	3

WEAPONS CONTINUED

Weapon Name	Range	Attack Dice	Special Rules	Build Slots	Cost
Rockets	Double	6D6	Ammo 3.	2	5
Sentry Gun	Dropped	2D6	Ammo 3. See special rules, page 80.	-	3
Shotgun	Long	*	Crew Fired. See special rules, page 77.	-	4
Smoke Dropper	Dropped	-	Ammo 3. See special rules, page 80.	-	1
Steel Nets	Short	(3D6)	Crew Fired. Blast. See special rules, page 77.	-	2
Submachine Gun	Medium	3D6	Crew fired.	-	5
Thumper	Medium	-	Ammo 1. Electrical. Indirect. 360-degree. See special rules, page 74.	2	4**
Wall of Amplifiers	Medium	-	360-degree Arc of Fire. See special rules, page 74.	3	4
Wreck Lobber	Double/Dropped	-	Ammo 3. See special rules, page 75.	4	4
Wrecking Ball	Short	*	*See special rules, page 76.	3	2

** Mishkin-sponsored teams only.

UPGRADES

Upgrades	Special Rules	Build Slots	Cost
Armour Plating	+2 Hull Points.	1	4
Experimental Nuclear Engine	Electrical. See special rules, page 83.	-	5**
Experimental Teleporter	Electrical. See special rules, page 83.	-	7**
Exploding Ram	Ammo 1. See special rules, page 84.	-	3
Extra Crewmember	+1 Crew, up to a maximum of twice the vehicle's starting Crew Value.	-	4
Improvised Sludge Thrower	See special rules, page 84.	1	2
Nitro Booster	Ammo 1. See special rules, page 84.	-	6
Ram	See special rules, page 85.	1	4
Roll Cage	See special rules, page 85.	1	4
Tank Tracks	-1 Max Gear. +1 Handling. See special rules, page 85.	1	4
Turret Mounting for Weapon	Weapon gains 360-degree arc of fire.	-	(x3)

** Mishkin-sponsored teams only.

BIKE — LIGHTWEIGHT

HULL □□
□□

FULL THROTTLE, PIVOT

MAX GEAR
6

HANDLING: 5   CREW: 1   CANS: ____

BUGGY — LIGHTWEIGHT

HULL □□□
□□□

ROLL CAGE

MAX GEAR
6

HANDLING: 4   CREW: 2   CANS: ____

CAR — MIDDLEWEIGHT

HULL □□□□□
□□□□□

MAX GEAR
5

HANDLING: 3   CREW: 2   CANS: ____

PERFORMANCE CAR — MIDDLEWEIGHT

HULL □□□□
□□□□

SLIP AWAY

MAX GEAR
6

HANDLING: 4   CREW: 1   CANS: ____

TRUCK — MIDDLEWEIGHT

HULL □□□□□
□□□□□

MAX GEAR
4

HANDLING: 2   CREW: 3   CANS: ____

MONSTER TRUCK — HEAVYWEIGHT

HULL □□□□□
□□□□□

ALL TERRAIN, UP AND OVER

MAX GEAR
4

HANDLING: 3   CREW: 2   CANS: ____

HEAVY TRUCK — HEAVYWEIGHT

HULL □□□□□□□
□□□□□□□

MAX GEAR
3

HANDLING: 2   CREW: 4   CANS: ____

BUS — HEAVYWEIGHT

HULL □□□□□□□□
□□□□□□□□

MAX GEAR
3

HANDLING: 2   CREW: 8   CANS: ____

BIKE WITH SIDECAR — LIGHTWEIGHT

HULL: ☐☐ / ☐☐

FULL THROTTLE, PIVOT

MAX GEAR: 6

HANDLING: 5   CREW: 2   CANS: ____

DRAG RACER — LIGHTWEIGHT

HULL: ☐☐ / ☐☐

JET ENGINE

MAX GEAR: 6

HANDLING: 4   CREW: 1   CANS: ____

GYROCOPTER — MIDDLEWEIGHT

HULL: ☐☐ / ☐☐

AIRWOLF, AIRBORNE

MAX GEAR: 6

HANDLING: 4   CREW: 1   CANS: ____

ICE-CREAM TRUCK — MIDDLEWEIGHT

HULL: ☐☐☐☐☐ / ☐☐☐☐☐

INFURIATING JINGLE

MAX GEAR: 4

HANDLING: 2   CREW: 2   CANS: ____

AMBULANCE — MIDDLEWEIGHT

HULL: ☐☐☐☐☐ / ☐☐☐☐☐

UPPERS, DOWNERS

MAX GEAR: 5

HANDLING: 2   CREW: 3   CANS: ____

HELICOPTER — HEAVYWEIGHT

HULL: ☐☐☐☐ / ☐☐☐☐

AIRWOLF, AIRBORNE

MAX GEAR: 4

HANDLING: 3   CREW: 3   CANS: ____

TANK — HEAVYWEIGHT

HULL: ☐☐☐☐☐☐☐☐☐☐ / ☐☐☐☐☐☐☐☐☐☐

PIVOT, ALL TERRAIN, UP AND OVER

MAX GEAR: 3

HANDLING: 4   CREW: 3   CANS: ____

WAR RIG — HEAVYWEIGHT

HULL: ☐☐☐☐☐☐☐☐☐☐☐☐ / ☐☐☐☐☐☐☐☐☐☐☐☐

ARTICULATED, PONDEROUS, PILEDRIVER

MAX GEAR: 4

HANDLING: 2   CREW: 5   CANS: ____

BUGGY
LIGHTWEIGHT

HULL ☐☐☐
☐☐☐

MAX GEAR
6

HANDLING: 4   CREW: 2   CANS: ____

CAR
MIDDLEWEIGHT

HULL ☐☐☐☐☐
☐☐☐☐☐

MAX GEAR
5

HANDLING: 3   CREW: 2   CANS: ____

TRUCK
MIDDLEWEIGHT

HULL ☐☐☐☐☐☐
☐☐☐☐☐☐

MAX GEAR
4

HANDLING: 2   CREW: 3   CANS: ____

PERFORMANCE CAR
MIDDLEWEIGHT

HULL ☐☐☐☐
☐☐☐☐

MAX GEAR
6

HANDLING: 4   CREW: 1   CANS: ____

HEAVY TRUCK
HEAVYWEIGHT

HULL ☐☐☐☐☐☐
☐☐☐☐☐☐

MAX GEAR
3

HANDLING: 2   CREW: 4   CANS: ____

BUS
HEAVYWEIGHT

HULL ☐☐☐☐☐☐☐
☐☐☐☐☐☐☐

MAX GEAR
3

HANDLING: 2   CREW: 8   CANS: ____

TYPE: _____   WEIGHT: _____

HULL ☐☐☐☐☐☐☐☐☐☐
☐☐☐☐☐☐☐☐☐☐

MAX GEAR

HANDLING: __   CREW: __   CANS: ____

TYPE: _____   WEIGHT: _____

HULL ☐☐☐☐☐☐☐☐☐☐
☐☐☐☐☐☐☐☐☐☐

MAX GEAR

HANDLING: __   CREW: __   CANS: ____

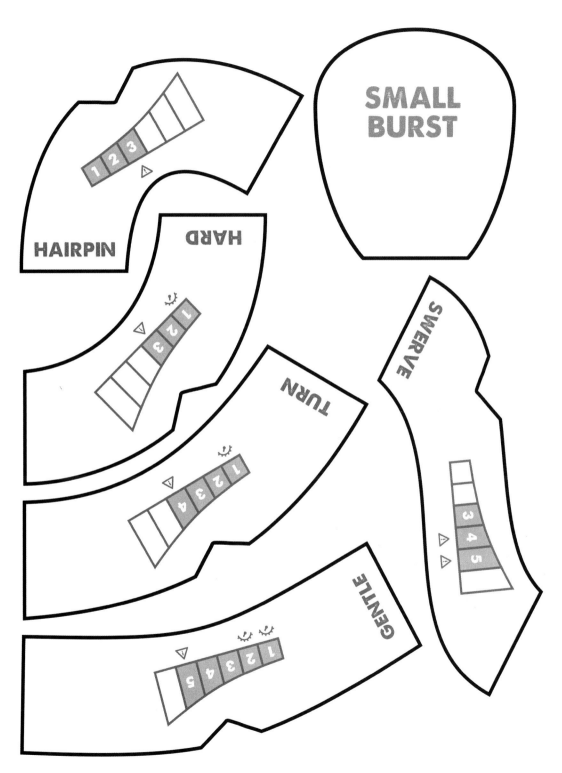

SMALL BURST

HAIRPIN

HARD

TURN

SWERVE

GENTLE

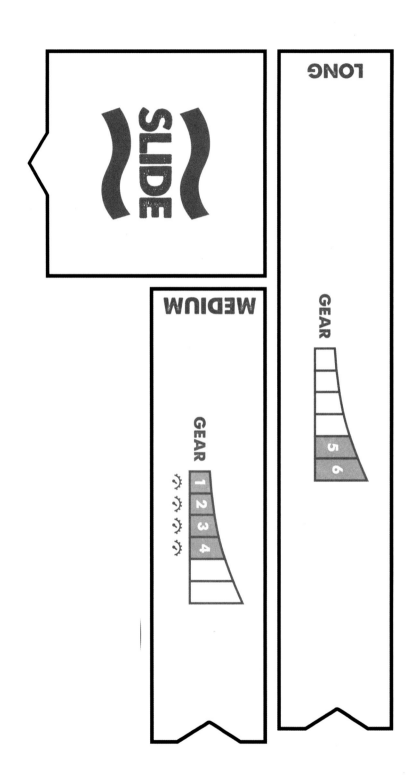

SHORT

1 2

VEER

2 3 4

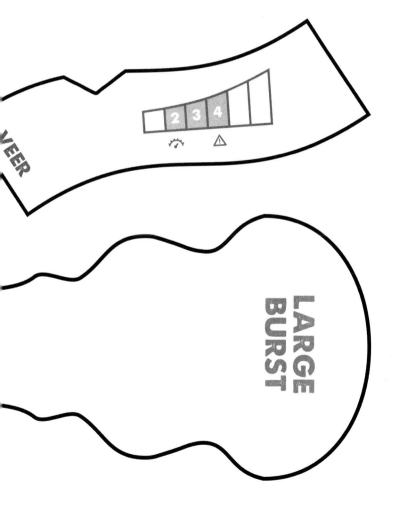

LARGE
BURST

HAZARD TOKEN   AMMO TOKEN   VOTE TOKEN

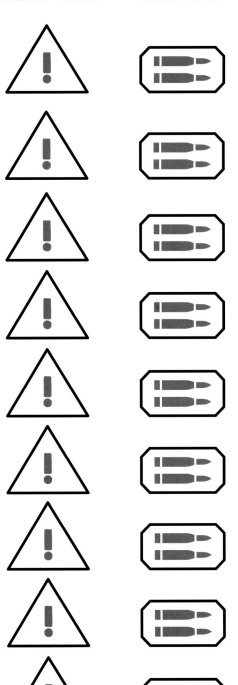